PRAISE FOR *REVIVAL IN THE ROCKIES*

"I'm confident this book will rivet your attention from the very first chapter, as it did mine. In this historical novel, Robert Allen uses many of the recorded facts of the day to weave a storyline of romance, revival, rodeo, and intrigue that stretches from Washington, DC, to the Rocky Mountains."

—RICK BROOKS, ministry representative, Word of Life International

"*Revival in the Rockies* is full of Montana lore—traditions, history, geography. But the connections between the possible new state governor, an old gold mine, the geyser basin in Yellowstone, and the FBI agent from Washington make it most intriguing."

—DOROTHY FREERKSEN, church librarian

"*Revival in the Rockies* describes a unique political race in Montana featuring a godly Native American candidate. The history and culture of the Reagan era provides the background. Humor, interesting characters, mystery, and adventure keep you guessing. Justice prevails only to provoke another twist in the plot. The romantic development of the key characters adds to the arresting nature of the book. It is a joy to recommend *Revival in the Rockies*."

—ERNIE SCHMIDT, former president, Faith Baptist Bible College and Seminary

"*Revival in the Rockies* moves the reader to greatly anticipate the next chapter while weaving historical facts throughout the story. There is no lack for the spiritual as you visit a local church ministry in the Rockies. An enjoyable and thought-provoking read!"

—ALAN POTTER, Shepherds Theological Seminary

"This well-written book is a page turner and lives up to its subtitle, *Politics, Rodeo, and Southern Gospel*. The historical novel takes place in Montana during the last of Jimmy Carter's presidency and the first term and re-election of Ronald Reagan. The book includes the intrigue of a thwarted terrorist attack, a talented award-winning Gospel quartet, a campaign for governor, and a captivating love story. Take up and read."

—GORDON TAYLOR, coordinator, Reformed Baptist Network

"Fans of Christian historical fiction will love this new twist on little-known Montana history. The descriptions of the vivid beauty of the Rockies, coupled with intriguing character development, produces a compelling story of patriotism, nostalgia, and a Gospel-centered love."

—BRETT WILLIAMS, Central Baptist Theological Seminary of Minneapolis

"The *New York Times* and H. L. Mencken free-associate the word revival more with Mississippi than Montana. Yet Montana is where Robert Allen leads his cast of characters. Other unlikely guest appearances are made by figures who have never yet come to mind in a Rorschach test concerning revival. Read. Be surprised. Enjoy."

—JAMES LUTZWEILER, former archivist, Southeastern Baptist Theological Seminary

"In his most recent novel, *Revival in the Rockies*, Robert Allen has skillfully woven a tale that combines the Big Sky Country of Montana, rodeos, and its Native American heritage with politics of the 1980s, the FBI, the ATF, and the message of the Gospel. The story draws you in and holds you to the very end. I enjoyed the book very much, and I believe you will too."

—JEFFREY TUTTLE, former dean, Calvary Baptist Theological Seminary

"In this third novel in his *Revival* series, Robert Allen hails back to his home state of Montana. As historical fiction set in the Reagan-era Cold War, this fascinating story has subplots involving Big Sky Country, Southern Gospel, rodeo, the FBI, Native American culture, and national, state, and local politics. Skillfully woven throughout is a love story pairing two unlikely suitors. I highly recommend this book!"

—RANDY MILLER, RESEARCH LIBRARIAN, Liberty University

REVIVAL in the ROCKIES

REVIVAL in the ROCKIES

Politics, Rodeo, and Southern Gospel

ROBERT A. ALLEN

RESOURCE *Publications* · Eugene, Oregon

REVIVAL IN THE ROCKIES
Politics, Rodeo, and Southern Gospel

Resource Publications
An Imprint of Wipf and Stock Publishers
199 W. 8th Ave., Suite 3
Eugene, OR 97401

www.wipfandstock.com

PAPERBACK ISBN: 978-1-6667-5200-7
HARDCOVER ISBN: 978-1-6667-5201-4
EBOOK ISBN: 978-1-6667-5202-1

07/18/22

FOR DOROTHY, PEGGY, AND DAVID

Who shared with me the joys and privileges of being preacher's kids!

"The course of true love never did run smooth."

WILLIAM SHAKESPEARE

ACKNOWLEDGMENTS

AMONG THE MANY RESOURCES providing historical material concerning the time period in which this novel has been set, none has been more valuable than the book *Tonight We Bombed the U.S. Capitol: The Explosive Story of M19, America's First Female Terrorist Group,* by William Rosenau. Published by Simon and Schuster, this book details the actions and results of the May 19th group over a period of several years. Rosenau demonstrates the accuracy of his history through copious footnotes and cross-references.

While using the information from this book, the author has taken the liberty of re-arranging some data to fit better with the time frame of his novel. For historical accuracy, reference should be made to the facts in the Rosenau volume. Any historical inaccuracies should be credited to the effort of this author to tell a story, based in a specific time period, but not necessarily correct in every historical detail.

Two other volumes which have been particularly useful in historical research have been *Montana, The Last Best Place,* published by the Montana Historical Society, and *Through Indian Eyes: The Untold Story of Native American People,* published by the Reader's Digest.

CHAPTER ONE

"Penny for Governor," shouted a self-appointed cheerleader as three hundred girls gathered for calisthenics on the lawn of Montana State University.

"Penny for Governor," echoed off the near-by mountains as a contingent of the girls took up the battle cry, transitioning into their city chant.

"A mile wide, an inch deep,
Too thick to plow, too thin to drink.
Powder River. Powder River. Go Powder River."

Girls cheered, screamed and hollered their political rally cry. Dressed in matching navy-blue shorts and powder blue t-shirts, they took full advantage of the opportunity presented by required morning calisthenics. Everyone gathered on the quad heard the enthusiastic support for their candidate.

A temperature of just under 50 degrees, and a brisk wind blowing down from the Gallatin Mountains still capped with snow, encouraged movement but discouraged talk. A gibbous moon shone down on the valley, challenging the rising sun to competition. Their excitement stemmed from the anticipation that one of their own Powder River Girl's Staters was running for Governor.

"Powder River. Powder River. Go Powder River," they shouted.

Scattered across the quad of the Montana State University campus in Bozeman, other groups of twenty-five to thirty exercised and listened to the rally cry. The mythical towns of Gallatin, Lewis and Clark, Yellowstone, Bear Tooth, Jefferson, and Madison joined Powder River to make up the Montana Girl's State participants. Most of the other towns' citizens worked out in silence, concentrating on the jumping jacks, dips, squats and crunches led by over-enthusiastic former Girl's Staters, now on staff. A few yelled catcalls and good-natured responses. With everyone gathered in one place, the girls from Powder River weren't about to let a chance like this get away.

"In for a Penny, in for a Pound," they shouted. "Get your money's worth. Penny for Governor. Time for Change."

Penny Whitman felt a slight blush color her face which had nothing to do with the heat of the exercises. She still couldn't get used to the idea that the other Native American high schoolers at the annual Girl's State event hosted by the American Legion Auxiliary decided she should receive the nomination for Governor. Her dark complexion helped hide the blush, but nothing could disguise the fact that she towered over the other girls. Being the tallest in her class since fourth grade had once been a source of vexation, but long legs proved useful on the rodeo circuit. Coal-black hair cascaded down her back as she jumped. The exercises may have been a necessary method of starting the day for many of the girls, but years of horseback riding and barrel racing toned her body to the place where burpees which caused others to gasp for breath didn't even make her sweat. Only the embarrassment of being the center of attention brought out the blush. Rodeo she could handle, politics remained new.

"People already know your name because of the rodeo," her friend and mentor Alicia Walks-Softly reminded her. "Name recognition remains pure gold in politics, especially here where you have only one week to campaign. Reigning as Queen of the Home of Champions Rodeo will be worth at least a hundred votes, believe me."

Alicia, one of the former Girl's Staters now on staff, had given every girl in the mythical city of Powder River a pocket full of pennies to distribute freely. The "In for a Penny, in for a Pound" slogan referred to Penny and her lieutenant-governor running mate, Elise Poundstone. Only a dozen or so Native American girls attended out of the more than three hundred Girl's Staters, but Penny's rodeo fame convinced them from the start that this year a Reservation Rising could happen. Seeing one of their own elected to the highest office in the state would qualify as a well-fought victory, almost equal to the defeat of General George Armstrong Custer at the Battle of the Little Big Horn. The fact that the Continental Divide Party nominated Liz Mitchell from Class A Billings West didn't discourage them, although Liz captained the West High cheer squad and claimed the title of Miss Montana earlier that summer.

Penny's supporters called their campaign the Big Sky Party, privately referring to Liz's followers as the Brownnosers. They appealed to every voter from any village smaller than Billings and Missoula to accept Penny for Change instead of allowing the big schools to continue their historical domination. Girl's State Governors always came from Butte, Missoula, or Billings. Those schools sent the largest delegations and assumed they deserved the honor. Class D schools like Plentywood and Elk Lodge had no business even trying to overthrow the established system in their exalted opinion, an opinion which no one asked for, but was still offered freely.

Earlier in the week elections for city and county officials maintained a low-key presence. No one even noticed Penny's election as mayor of Powder River. Everything changed with the nomination for Governor. The *Billings Gazette* and even the *Denver Post* ran feature articles on the upcoming gubernatorial campaign. Reporters focused attention on the urban-rural divide and Native American success scenario posed by her candidacy. No one used the politically incorrect term "noble savage," but the articles abounded with assurances that Montanans considered their first settlers equal to the later-arriving white men in every way.

Alicia fell in step with Penny as they walked back to the dormitories to change clothes in preparation for the morning lecture series. Each day a charismatic professor from Midland Christian College in Midland, Texas, presented a series on anti-communism called "The Battle Ahead."

"Nothing to worry about," Alicia assured her. "Even the Billings and Missoula delegations show signs of splitting right down the middle. No one really likes Liz. And they don't want to be seen as racist for voting against an Arapaho, even if she is half-Irish. Not even an October surprise could keep you out of the governorship at this late date. Victory lies within our grasp."

Penny smiled. "I think it would hurt you more than it would me if I lost, Alicia. You're the one who deserves all the credit for this campaign. I would just as soon be on Jupiter racing around barrels rather than facing reporters. At least I know how the barrels and my horse will react. Reporters? Unpredictable! Politics? Terrifying!"

"Reporters remain my problem, not yours, sweetie. Just keep smiling and shaking hands and making promises you'll never need to keep because Girl's State lasts only one week. Let me take care of the rest."

In spite of Alicia's reassurance, an October surprise did arrive that very morning in the form of an article in the *Girl's State Gazette* distributed to every delegate as they exited the lectures.

"Could Whitman Be A Bad Penny?" screamed the headline, warning of even greater revelations to come.

"Recent information resulting from the investigative work of *Gazette* staffers sheds new light on the campaign for Governor at Montana Girl's State. A trustworthy source with ties to the inner circle of the notorious anti-government Native Resistance Movement suggests there may be more to the success of Penny Whitman than meets the eye."

"For the past several years government agents have been watching closely the activities of the so-called Native Resistance Movement. The group's publicly stated goal involves encouraging Native Americans to participate in local elections in order to improve the living conditions on the reservations in Montana, Wyoming and Idaho. That goal hides their ultimate objective of rebellion and secession, revival of Native dominance over the entire region. They often refer to the three-state area in their private correspondence as Wy-ho-tana. The roots of the movement date back to the Absaroka Statehood agitation of 1939 led by A. R. Swickard of Sheridan, Wyoming. Absaroka is a Crow word meaning 'children of the large-beaked bird.' Various government agencies, including Alcohol, Tobacco and Firearms, have discovered caches of rifles and ammunition in hunting campsites throughout the area thought to be held in reserve for the initiation of their armed rebellion. To the amazement of everyone it has come to light that the ranch owned and operated by Penny Whitman's father, Lee, is called Ab-Sa-Ro-Ka. The ranch sits exactly on the border of the three states claimed by NRM: Montana, Wyoming, and Idaho."

All across campus girls gathered in small groups reading and reacting.

"It's all lies," fumed Alicia. "No evidence at all. Who's the trustworthy source? Who even wrote the article? There's no by-line."

"It's all right," Penny shrugged. "The girls here are smart. They will see that it's simply condemnation by association. I've never even heard of the Native Resistance Movement."

"How could the *Gazette* sponsors even allow the article to be published? It's just a bunch of garbage." Alicia crumpled her copy of the *Gazette* into a ball. "I bet Liz wrote this. She couldn't put her name on it because then everyone would know she's perpetrating a fraud. That's why there's no by-line. I swear she would pull a Charles Colson and walk over her own grandmother to win this election."

"It won't be the first time for the media to show favoritism in a political campaign." Penny folded up her copy of the paper and looked over the quad crowded with fellow Girl's Staters. "Give everyone some credit, Alicia. Trustworthy sources don't refuse to give their names. Just let it go."

The distribution of pennies by the Powder River girls continued unabated right on through the picnic dinner served to the delegates that evening. From many of the conversations, it appeared as if the article simply heightened interest in Penny's campaign. Questions from her fellow delegates ranged from serious to ludicrous.

"Does your father's ranch really cover all three states?"

One of the Billings girls who had probably never visited a ranch made it sound like Lee Whitman had already taken over the leadership of the Wy-ho-tana movement, reigning over the entire area.

Penny smiled sweetly. "Ab-Sa-Ro-Ka Ranch borders Wyoming and Idaho, but we own land only in Montana. You do realize that Montana has a longer border than any other state except Texas and Alaska?"

A voice from the edge of the crowd of girls shouted loud enough for everyone to hear. "Were you raised on the reservation?"

She tried to see who had asked the question, so she could smile at her like Alicia instructed, but the girl faded into the crowd.

"Nope." Penny smiled instead at those close by. "Dad and Mom moved to the ranch just outside of Elk Lodge before I was born."

"Do you hunt with a bow and arrow?" This girl stood close enough that Penny could answer with not only a smile, but a twinkle in her eyes.

"Occasionally, but I'm much better with a 30.06. Last year I harvested both deer and elk. Looking forward to hunting season this fall."

"Are you really a full-blooded Arapaho?"

"Half Arapaho and half Irish, but all American. Dad's parents still live on the reservation. Mom's ancestors came from County Kent in Ireland. The Arapahos prefer to call themselves Big Sky People, just like all of us Montanans who live in Big Sky Country."

The anonymous voice shouted again, "Have you ever counted coup?"

Penny laughed and shouted back. "I've never even worked in a hair salon. Do you need a trim?"

JUST BEFORE MIDNIGHT ONE of the Girl's State sponsors knocked on the door of the room Liz Mitchell shared with another delegate from Billings.

"Liz? We just received a call from Deaconess Hospital in Billings. Your mother has been admitted with a massive heart attack. They suggest you return home immediately."

Alicia Walks-Softly watched from the shadow of a large elm tree as the faculty sponsor from West High School helped Liz into a car which headed east toward Billings. It had proved easy to impersonate a nurse over the telephone. No one even thought to check back with the hospital on the authenticity of the message. Liz wasn't the only one capable of producing an October surprise, she thought. If Liz wanted to play in the big leagues, the time had come to up her game. You didn't mess with Alicia Walks-Softly and avoid a counterattack. She grinned to herself as she walked back to the dormitory. Walks-Softly and Carries a Big Stick. Teddy Roosevelt would have been proud of her.

Three hundred girls read the article about Penny in the *Girl's State Gazette* on Thursday. Three hundred girls walked to the polls on the campus of Montana State Friday afternoon. Those planning all week to vote for Penny

Whitman carried their pennies with them and voted the Big Sky ticket. Those planning all week to vote against her candidacy, marked their ballots accordingly. One delegate, who had made a late-night trip to Billings only to find her mother in perfect health, didn't get back to Bozeman in time to vote. The ticket of Penny and Pound won by a landslide.

CHAPTER TWO

"Welcome to Face the Nation. Today we have a guest from ATF, the Alcohol, Tobacco and Firearms Division. Judson Freeborn has been with the agency since its inception in 1972 as an independent bureau within the Treasury Department."

The host of the longest running news show in television history flashed a grin across the table toward his guest before continuing the introduction. Freeborn returned the gesture with a confident smile.

"If you find yourself unfamiliar with ATF, think Eliot Ness and the Untouchables. These guys represent the oldest tax collection agency of the federal government. They enforced Prohibition, drove Joe Camel off television, and find themselves currently tasked with protecting us from home-grown terrorism. Which brings us to our topic for today. International Terrorism."

The host stopped for a drink from his coffee cup, turning away from the camera toward his guest. "Judson, this morning marks the 222nd day since the Muslim Student Followers of the Imam's Line captured the United States Embassy in Tehran, taking fifty-two hostages. The entire nation has been following this crisis, cheering when Canada rescued the six American diplomats who had evaded capture, and despairing over the failure of Operation Eagle Claw."

Judson nodded solemnly, waiting for the inevitable question.

"Recently, at the Republican National Convention, William Casey, campaign manager for Governor Ronald Reagan, exploded a political bombshell when he suggested that President Carter may be stalling negotiations in order to revive his tepid campaign with an October surprise. Mr. Freeborn, what was your reaction to Mr. Casey's accusation? Are we indeed in line for another October surprise?"

"Thank you for inviting me to be here today."

Judson Freeborn, a veteran of the Washington talk-show circuit, leaned in toward the microphone and focused his attention on the camera rather than on his host. An unruly thatch of hair failed to detract from the sophisticated look of a youthful figure in a pin-stripe suit. Intense eyes with a touch of blue gazed through the camera as if looking directly into the faces of those watching the program in their living rooms. A careful application of Max Factor pancake foundation prevented the pale, death-like appearance with which Richard Nixon struggled during the Nixon-Kennedy debates a few years earlier. Television interviews had come a long way since that time.

"Well, we certainly don't expect any surprise of the magnitude of what happened back in 1912," Judson began. "That was the year Theodore Roosevelt became the target of an assassination attempt in Milwaukee, Wisconsin. Upon hearing the report of the gun, he reached into his inner pocket, pulled out his fifty-page speech manuscript dripping with blood, and proceeded to deliver the entire speech beginning with these words. 'I don't know whether you fully understand that I have just been shot, but it takes more than that to kill a bull moose.'"

The host laughed. "No, we certainly hope that no idiot will take pot shots at either Governor Reagan or President Carter. I was thinking more in terms of the stupid remark made by that Presbyterian preacher back in 1884 about the Democrats being the party of 'rum, Romanism and rebellion.' That one cost James G. Blaine the election, didn't it?"

"That's what historians have concluded.," agreed Judson. "Blaine failed to disclaim the remark until after he became known as a Catholic hater. Grover Cleveland won New York and the presidency with the support of Irish Catholics. I really don't think that Mr. Casey's comment rises to the level of that incident. The President has handled the negotiations with Iran so inefficiently that nothing between now and November could convince the American people that he should be re-elected."

"Not even if it became known that the Republican candidate was actually the one delaying the release of the hostages? Was Casey providing a red herring?"

"Ridiculous." Freeborn turned away from the camera and stared into the eyes of his interviewer, challenging him to prove the accusation.

"Listen to this." The host pulled an article out of a file on the desk in front of him and began to read.

"According to Robert Dreyfuss, Reagan advisor Henry Kissinger met with the Iranians on several occasions. The offer was made to release Iranian money frozen in New York banks and provide weapons to the Iranians, which they need for their war with Iraq. In exchange, Khomeini would deliver the hostages after the election instead of prior to November."

Judson shrugged casually, glad that he had prepared well for the interview.

"I am familiar with your source. This is just another conspiracy theory promulgated by none other than Lyndon LaRouche in his *Executive Intelligence Review*."

Turning back toward the camera, he addressed the listening audience directly. "In the interest of fairness, it is only right to inform your listeners that LaRouche supports socialism and Marxism. He's a communist, so of course he would oppose a conservative like Governor Reagan. It's because of men like Lyndon LaRouche that we need a strong voice for conservatism here in Washington."

Setting the article aside, the commentator focused his attention once again on his guest.

"You will have to admit, however, that the Governor has access to the same intelligence briefings conducted regularly for President Carter. He has knowledge of everything the government has been doing to try to resolve this dilemma for 222 days. Inside information which you and I do not share."

"Nothing unusual about that." Judson answered, looking directly into the camera once again. "Providing access to information remains a customary practice in a nation committed to democratic principles and the smooth transition of power. To the best of my knowledge such access has been granted to major party candidates for many years. No matter who wins an election, that person needs to be well informed concerning the status of foreign affairs. He needs to be ready to govern on day one."

"So, the Governor would know in advance what diplomatic maneuvers have been attempted by the Carter administration. His man Kissinger would also know."

Judson smiled. "As would every one of the President's cabinet members, his press secretary, and every staff member of every member of the House and Senate Intelligence committees. I dare say that even the student interns know. There are no secrets in Washington."

The host smiled, satisfied that he had stirred up enough controversy to increase viewer ratings.

"Thank you, Judson. Let me turn to a happier topic. I understand that your son will be graduating from the FBI Academy later this week."

Judson relaxed slightly. He couldn't think of any way this part of the interview could become controversial.

"He will. Ron has completed his initial weeks of training and will walk the line on Saturday along with the latest class of agents."

"And, if my information is correct, as the youngest FBI recruit in the history of the Academy."

Judson grinned. "He won't be happy to have you mention that, but yes. Marilyn and I are very proud of his accomplishment. Ron completed his undergraduate degree at age nineteen and spent two years in Israel as assistant to the ambassador at the embassy in Tel Aviv. He speaks both Hebrew and Russian fluently which is the reason the FBI recruited him in the first place."

"And granted him the age exemption. I understand he also excels on the piano. Is there anything he can't do?"

"Well, according to his mother he's not very good at writing regular letters home when he's out of the country," Judson laughed. "He played Shostakovich's *Piano Concerto No. 2* with the Jerusalem Symphony Orchestra during his years in Israel. So, I guess excel would be an appropriate descriptor. Thankfully he did let his mother know about that concert. We were able to attend along with his mentor Helen Forrester."

"Congratulations are certainly in order, Judson. Thank you again for joining us this morning on Face the Nation."

"It has been my privilege."

CHAPTER THREE

"DO YOU REALLY THINK Ronald Reagan can unseat a sitting President?" Penny Whitman turned off the television in the living-room of her ranch home as the broadcast of Face the Nation concluded. "I haven't paid much attention to the national news, but your uncle sure seems to think it is a done deal."

Cynthia Freeborn grinned. "He knows what he's talking about. Uncle Jud has worked in Washington all his life. And now Ron's with the FBI. If they think Reagan can win, you can be mighty sure it will happen. The polls here in Montana show him leading Carter by twelve points."

"It was fun to hear them talking about an October surprise. I didn't even know what an October surprise was when Alicia started predicting one at Girl's State last year. Guess I'd better bone up on my political history before I serve as a staff member in Bozeman this summer."

"Alicia would know. And I'm learning. Just ask me anything," laughed Cynthia. "Anything about national politics, that is. Montana's still a mystery. It's a good thing our debate topics are chosen at the national level rather than in state."

"It's a deal. You unveil the mystery of national politics to me, and I'll show you the open book of the Big Sky. Rodeo from me and politics from you. What do you say we begin with a trail ride up toward the Continental Divide while you lecture me on current events?"

The arrival of James Freeborn in Elk Lodge, Montana, to start a new church earlier that summer led to an immediate friendship between Penny and Cynthia. Penny discovered the church services held in the basement of the town library through a poster in the upper floor reading room. The fact that Cynthia stopped to post the sign when she came to subscribe for a library card had been providential. Meeting Penny compensated in some degree for the friendships left behind in Ohio. Being accepted like another daughter into the Freeborn household gave Penny not only a sister, but a mother-figure to replace the one she had never known.

In return, Penny's father Lee nearly adopted Cynthia. His ranch became her second home, introducing her to the west through a total immersion in a culture she had never before experienced. Horses and cattle. Fishing and hunting. Riding fence. Branding and rodeos. Cynthia's only regret remained the fact that Lee wouldn't come to church despite her effort to encourage him in that direction.

"Why would I look for God in the basement of a library," he would say. "He's out here in the mountains where I don't have to search for Him. Our people found spiritual strength in our dreams and visions and sacred objects long before the white man ever set foot on this side of the great river. Your people talk about finding God as if you have somehow lost Him. The Arapaho never lost Him. A shaman named Sword once said, 'Every object in the world has a spirit and that spirit is Wakan. These Wakan beings are greater than mankind in the same way that mankind is greater than animals. They can do many things that mankind cannot do. Mankind can pray to the Wakan beings for help.' Doesn't that sound like the God you white people seem to have lost? Maybe if you spend enough time up in the Rockies, you'll find him there."

"Will you be riding Jupiter today?" Cynthia asked as they walked toward the barn to saddle up for the trail ride.

"Nah. Can't risk injuring him on the rough paths up toward the Divide. We'll take Betsy and Sundance. You remember Wicasa Walks-Softly, don't you? He'll help you with the saddle but watch closely, because tacking up needs to be one of your first lessons in becoming a westerner."

The Camas flowers which dotted the meadow with their explosions of white and pink soon gave way to smaller yellow and red wildflowers as the trail's elevation increased. Snow still capped the peaks of the Gallatin Range while white reservoirs of drifts clung tightly to the north-facing canyons.

"You've never told me what brought your family to Montana."

As the horses entered a highland meadow, Penny waited for Cynthia to ride alongside for a time, something which had been impossible on the narrow trail.

"It's not something we talk about much," said Cynthia. "I think it was probably one of the hardest trials Dad has ever faced. We're all glad to be here now, but it wasn't what we would have chosen at the time. It all goes back to politics, so I guess this is your first lesson."

"Seems fair enough since we've been enjoying the Big Sky I promised in exchange for your wisdom" Penny teased.

"The church Dad pastored in Ohio experienced exceptional growth. We completed a new auditorium which seated eight hundred and it was already full. Everyone seemed to love him and his preaching. But then he invited a singing group to come called the "Sounds of Liberty." Have you heard of Jerry Falwell?"

"Old Time Gospel Hour? Of course. That was my television church before your father came to town."

"Well, the Sounds concert drew a great crowd, and nothing really political occurred. But then Dr. Falwell started the Moral Majority which strongly advocated the Reagan presidential campaign. Unions dominate the culture in Toledo. The main businesses include auto assembly plants and glass manufacturing. A small group of influential men in the church decided Dad no longer deserved their pulpit. Rather than fight the inevitable, he resigned and came here."

"But why Elk Lodge? No one outside of Montana has ever heard of this town."

"That's where the entire story got interesting. A former college friend of Dad's who now lives in Laurel knew a couple in Elk Lodge who had been praying for a church. You know the Bledsoes. They were the only people we knew when we came."

"Wow. Wasn't it C.S. Lewis who said, 'Pain is God's megaphone'? That must have been really hard on your father."

"For sure. But after we had been here a few weeks, he told us in family devotions that becoming so busy with the work in Ohio prevented him from making time for a closer relationship with God. He needed to rest, and God had to force him to realize that. He loves it here in Montana, and so do we all."

"Even Will?"

"Even Will. The first time your father took him fishing and he hooked a Rainbow Trout with a fly he had personally tied, he was hooked on the west. I just wish we could get Uncle Judson and Marilyn and Ron to come out for a visit. They would love it too."

As the trail narrowed once again, conversation became impossible. Instead, the girls rode quietly, isolated from civilization, but enveloped by the majesty of the mountains. Cynthia certainly understood her father's remarks about finding peace. It made perfect sense, just like the observation Penny's father Lee often shared.

"If God, or Wakan, doesn't live in Montana, at least He comes here on vacation."

CHAPTER FOUR

THE GOAL OF GRADUATING from the FBI Academy became a fixation in the mind of Ron Freeborn long before he even became a teenager. He read every book he could find about the history of the Bureau and watched the classic 1935 James Cagney film "G Men" more times than he could count. His mother ordered the "I Spy" kit advertised in *Mad* Magazine for his eighth birthday, and the little score cards where he kept track of every item he spied filled in quickly. Even the two years in Israel had been part of the preparation. Two years of practical experience, in addition to a college degree, remained basic requirements for the FBI Academy. His flair for languages and musical talent proved to recruiters that he possessed a well-rounded background. Years of hard study and practice finally paid off, although he would be the first to admit that both languages and music came easy for him.

Today his dream of a lifetime would come true.

The nearly two hundred graduates of the current agent training class competed against thousands of applicants just to enroll. Seventeen weeks of intensive study and physical training pushed their minds and bodies to the limit. Ethics, behavioral training, forensic science, writing, and investigative techniques taught in the classroom stretched their intellect. Self-defense skills, firearms training, disarming techniques, searches of subjects, handcuffing, boxing, and safe driving honed their physical skills in the field. Real-life scenarios with paint guns prepared them for bank robberies, kidnappings, assaults with a deadly weapon, and armed arrests. The threat of terrorist attacks became very real with the escalation of the Cold War, the emergence of Al Fatah, and the Popular Front for the Liberation of Palestine.

The failure of elite troops to rescue the fifty-two Iranian hostages back in April further intensified the importance of their training. The entire nation seemed stuck in a malaise, relieved only by the victory of the U.S.A. hockey team over the Russians at Lake Placid during the Winter Olympics in February. Intensely patriotic, Ron took personally the loss of the eight servicemen in Operation Eagle Claw. He resented the presidential decision to abort the operation, and the Ayatollah Khomeini's claim that angels of God had foiled the mission. Now his active involvement in the protection of the nation he loved stood ready to become a reality.

FBI Director William Webster presided over the ceremony, attended by friends and family. Each graduate, as always, received a badge and credentials. Special honors awaited outstanding achievement in academics, firearms, and physical fitness. Dream sheets of duty stations where each agent desired to be assigned had been submitted. For Ron, that meant Washington, D.C., the location of FBI headquarters and the place of action.

Each graduate received three tickets to the ceremony. Ron's went to his parents, Judson and Marilyn, and long-time family friend and piano teacher Helen Forrester. He knew they shared his excitement, although Helen hoped after the gig with the Jerusalem Symphony Orchestra that he might dedicate his future to music instead of law enforcement.

"Ready to shake the Director's hand when he gives you the academic award?"

Ron's roommate Tim Fusco finished tying his four-in-hand, sliding the knot up tight against the collar of his dress shirt. "Sure glad we only have to wear these suits for graduation."

"You can say that again. But don't." Ron added the last when Tim opened his mouth to repeat the phrase, one of their favorite inside jokes. "Suits and ties and summer in Virginia don't mix. As far as any awards go, I'll just be glad to get the badge. You're the one who will be up there shaking Webster's hand. Crack-shot Fusco."

He wrestled with his own tie, checking in the mirror to make sure the knot was snug. How his grade-point average compared with others remained a mystery, but everyone in the Academy knew that Tim Fusco could shoot a bee off the top of a flower without ever disturbing the petals.

The two of them headed out the door and across the parade grounds toward the new auditorium where graduation would take place. Hundreds of visitors, and the other members of their class streamed toward the site. Dress suits abounded despite the temperature, so the two men who approached them from the opposite direction didn't attract undue attention. The greatest difference came from the identical Ray-Bans covering their eyes and the small lapel pin each man wore.

"Ron Freeborn?" The two stopped in front of them on the sidewalk. One of them stepped aside to allow Tim to continue, making it clear that they had no business with him.

"Yes? I'm Ron."

"Come with us please."

"Webster probably wants you on the platform after that plug your dad gave you on Face the Nation," suggested Tim, bowing as if greeting a celebrity. "See you later."

Taking a position on either side of him, the two Secret Service agents guided him unobtrusively toward a nearby office building. Once inside they directed him to a straight-backed chair in an empty waiting room. The men remained standing.

"Mr. Freeborn. When you applied to the FBI you agreed to come under the ultimate authority of the Commander in Chief, just as if you joined one of the military branches. In accordance with orders from the highest echelon of executive authority in the United States of America, it has become our duty to inform you of the following."

The taller of the two men pulled an envelope from an inner pocket and unfolded a letter. Ron spotted the imprint of the White House address even before they handed him the missive.

"By order of the President of the United States," he read. "Ronald Freeborn is hereby relieved of all duty and responsibility relating to the Federal Bureau of Investigation."

The letter was jerked from his hand before he could read the signature.

Ron looked at the two men, trying, and failing to read the expression on faces seemingly etched from granite.

"I don't understand."

The taller of the two men reinserted the letter into the envelope and returned it to his inner pocket. "Your duty requires that you return to your room, pack up all belongings and absent yourself from Quantico before the conclusion of today's exercises. One of us will escort you to the dormitory. A military vehicle will be waiting at the gate in fifteen minutes to provide transport."

Inside the auditorium the graduation exercises continued uninterrupted. A few people noticed that the award for highest academic achievement noted in the program failed to be conferred. A few more wondered why Gaus followed Fraile onto the platform to receive his badge and credentials when the name Freeborn clearly appeared between them on the official list of graduates. They all applauded when Crack-shot Fusco accepted the award for Firearms Expertise. Only Helen and the Freeborns seemed to realize that something had gone terribly wrong. Ron was missing.

The agents accompanying Ron said nothing as they walked back to his dormitory room to collect his belongings. He knew the men provided as escorts simply fulfilled duties to which they had been assigned, so questioning them would prove futile. Supervisors and faculty members occupied seats in the auditorium for the ceremony unavailable for any appeal. Besides, who had enough authority to overturn a mandate by the Commander in Chief?

He could not remember a single time before in his entire life when he had not been excited to be alive. Fulfillment always exceeded anticipation. Performing with the Jerusalem Symphony far excelled the triumph of winning the Paderewski competition. FBI Graduation held the promise of exultation beyond any joy of acceptance into or training from the Bureau. Never before had failure proved to be the end result of any personal endeavor. Never before had failure to succeed provided disappointment as a climax for hard work.

As kids, he and his cousins used a standard retort for the complaint, "Life's not fair."

"Tough."

"What's tough?"

"Life."

"What's life?

"*Life's* a magazine."

"How much does it cost?

"Twenty cents."

"I only have a nickel."

"Tough."

Somehow that chant failed to provide the comfort he sought. After a lifetime of unmitigated light, it seemed that he plunged into total darkness, as one of his favorite poets, James Weldon Johnson, would say, "blacker than a hundred midnights down in the cypress swamp." What could he possibly have done wrong to be stripped of all duty and responsibility before even receiving his badge? He felt old, as if aging ten years in the last fifteen minutes. Anticipation of fulfillment and success receded into bitterness and woe. The gates closing behind him blocked access to the path walked since childhood. The Jeep waiting for him symbolized exile and even imprisonment. Success turned aside, a future torn away, his very soul ripped to pieces. Someone made him their target and scored a bullseye. His fellow recruits would ridicule him. Taunts would inhabit his nightmares. Music would vanish out of his life.

The trip to his parent's house passed in silence. The driver didn't even ask for an address. His orders came from higher up. Pulling into the Freeborn driveway, he helped Ron unload his pack and drove away without saying a word.

CHAPTER FIVE

JUDSON, MARILYN, AND HELEN approached Tim in the receiving line as soon as possible, not wanting to take him away from his well-wishers. Even so, Judson interrupted a couple who wanted to know what weapons had been included in the training as well as types of ammunition, distances from targets and frequency of visits to the rifle range.

"I can't imagine what happened to Ron," Tim told them. "We were walking over here from the dorm when two men met him, and insisted he go somewhere with them. I really thought that they were taking him backstage to have him join the celebrities on the platform. I'm sure you noticed that they skipped right over the award for academic excellence. We all knew none of us could compete with his brain. His grades made that achievement a shoo-in."

"And that's the last you saw of him?" Marilyn's calm manner provided a stark contrast to her husband's intensity.

"Absolutely. I only became aware of his absence when they skipped that award. I wish I could tell you more."

"Do you mind if we check out your room?" Judson edged away, nodding in the direction of the dorms.

"Not at all. I'd go with you but. . ." He glanced over their shoulders at the others who were waiting to congratulate him.

"No problem. I know where it is. Thanks Tim. And good job."

Nothing in the dorm room gave any indication that anyone other than Tim Fusco had ever lived there. Even the government issued bedding had been stripped from the second bed. Marilyn and Helen watched as Judson searched for any clue to indicate Ron had occupied the room for the past weeks.

"People don't just disappear," said Marilyn.

"They do in Washington," came her husband's tense reply.

It was Helen who noticed the clipping about an upcoming National Symphony Orchestra concert at the Kennedy Center. Other items on the bulletin board included pictures of Tim's family, his girlfriend, and articles about the Washington Redskins.

"Did Tim strike you as someone who would be making plans to attend events at the Kennedy Center?" she asked.

Judson ripped the clipping right off the board. "You're right, Helen. Just makes me all the more certain this was deliberate. I only hope he's safe."

Marilyn gently removed the article from her husband's grasp and tacked it back up on the bulletin board. "Now, Judson. Don't borrow trouble. Let's go home and see if he's there. There must be some logical explanation."

What greeted them at the Freeborn residence proved both reassuring and disturbing. Even before they opened the doors of the car after pulling into the driveway, they heard the sound of the grand piano from the living room.

"Gustav Holst," whispered Helen. "*Mars, the Bringer of War.*"

The percussive rhythms and melodies, designed to stir the emotions, nearly vibrated the porch as the three of them stood and listened from outside. Anguish, frustration, and resentment poured from Ron's fingers into the keys, resounding through the strings and sounding board, engulfing them in his despair.

"Let him finish," encouraged Helen as Judson reached for the handle of the door. "The war is within."

Judson nodded, opening the door quietly and holding it for the ladies as they filed into the living room and became an audience of three. So engrossed in his music that he didn't even see them enter, Ron transformed the orchestral score, originally written as a two-piano arrangement into a *tour-de-force* of his own choosing. Mars in motion from the mind of Holst morphing into the melody borrowed by Williams for *The Imperial March* from *Star Wars*. Mars' potential for savagery echoed from the chords and progressions until the final bombast of the *March* ended and the sound of silence prevailed.

Helen finally broke that silence with a subdued quotation from Holst himself. "In the real world the end is not happy at all."

Ron rose from the bench, and bowed, a practice Helen had drilled into him from the time of his very first recital. Then he found himself engulfed in a mother's hug.

"It all happened so quickly," he explained. "Tim and I were on our way to the graduation when they came out of nowhere. Caught me totally by surprise."

"Did you ask for identification?" Judson knew his son was hurting, but fell back on what he knew best, procedure.

"They wore Secret Service lapel pins. The letter certainly seemed official."

"Letter?"

"From the White House. Signed by the President. At least, I think it was. They didn't let me keep it."

"They didn't announce an award for academic achievement." His mother pulled him down next to her on the couch and wouldn't release his hand. "That was our first clue."

"The award doesn't matter. It's the badge and the credentials. What am I going to do now?"

"The White House," repeated Judson. "This entire fiasco finally begins to make sense. This may all be my fault, son. I'm afraid the President decided there's not room for another Freeborn in government service."

"That's ridiculous," said Marilyn. "Even if he didn't like your interview on Face the Nation, he wouldn't take it out on Ron."

"Stranger things have happened in Washington. Becoming Chief Executive of the most powerful nation on earth often infuses average men with sovereign expectations. The fact that they can do anything convinces them that they should do anything. I'm sorry, Ron. You could put in an appeal to Webster, but if this came from the White House there's not a lot even the FBI Director can do."

"I don't blame you, Dad. It's just that joining the FBI has been my focus since before I can remember. I don't know what to do next."

His mother pulled him close, as if he were eight, and shed the tears he was too much of a man to release.

"I could request an appointment with the President," fumed Judson. "It's not right. There must be some channel of appeal. I have some contacts in the Secret Service. I could start with those."

"I have a suggestion." Helen had remained quiet through the description of the events at Quantico, listening, and thinking. "It may sound strange, Ron, but it would get you out of Washington and give you time to re-evaluate future plans. My father used to tell me that you should never make important decisions when you are flat on your back."

"Back to Jerusalem?" Despite his disappointment, Ron managed a smile, knowing his piano teacher would like nothing better than to see him follow her dream for his life. First the Paderewski competition, then Chopin in Geneva, Tchaikovsky in Moscow, and Queen Elizabeth in Brussels. Performances with the Vienna Philharmonic, the Budapest Festival Orchestra, and the Boston Pops.

"Not really. More like back to Joplin, Denver, and Sacramento," said Helen.

"Join the Army and see the world? Does the Army need a pianist?"

"Much better than the Army." Helen walked over to the keyboard and played a riff from the Imperials, top-of-the-charts gospel song *I'm Forgiven*. "I've been working with a quartet this summer. They traveled last school year for my alma mater and would like to make the transition to performing full-time on the road. They are good enough in my estimation. I have been helping with their itinerary which has filled rapidly. But their pianist decided to go to graduate school."

"A quartet?"

"Actually, a Southern Gospel Quartet. I know how much you enjoy the Blackwoods and that Whitey Gleason record, *Mr. Piano*. I bet you could still play *The Assurance March* just like you did in your fourth-grade recital."

Ron laughed and walked over to the piano. Turning back toward his parents he introduced himself in his best little boy voice. "My name is Ron Freeborn and today I am going to play *The Assurance March*."

When he finished, he took another bow as the three audience members applauded. "What are they called?" he asked Helen.

"The *Certain Sounds*. It comes from that verse in I Corinthians, 'if the trumpet give an uncertain sound, who shall prepare himself to the battle.'"

CHAPTER SIX

RON MANAGED ONE REHEARSAL with the quartet before they gave their next concert in Annapolis, Maryland. He could sightread the music. The casual church atmosphere provided a welcome contrast to the intensity of the Jerusalem Symphony and the FBI Academy. The fellows in the quartet, and the crowd, all loved *The Assurance March*.

"As good as Whitey Gleason," proclaimed one of the elderly gentlemen who greeted him after the service. "I just love to hear the great old hymns of the faith."

Roger Bosco, Les Frank, Niles Jensen, and Brook Wilson had sung together for the first time in chapel their freshman year in college. Recruited after graduation to represent their alma mater in churches across the nation, they enjoyed the experience so much that they decided to stay on the road. The fact that Helen Forrester served as an adjunct faculty member, taught their former pianist, and volunteered to oversee their itinerary during their first year of travel provided them with instant confidence that her choice for a new accompanist would be satisfactory. Ron did not disappoint.

The next night he did an arrangement of *When the Saints Go Marching In* that had the crowd on their feet cheering and applauding. From then on, every concert featured at least two and sometimes as many as five of his piano solos.

When the quartet sang in churches, the evening ended with a short sermon. Brook Wilson, a Bible major with plans to eventually go on to seminary, did the preaching.

"Any one of us could deliver his sermons. He only has two. We've heard them so many times we have them memorized," said Niles as they drove north toward their next stop in Baltimore.

Niles Jensen established himself as the navigator of the group and always sat in the front, calling "Shotgun" every time they loaded up for a trip.

He stuffed the jockey box with maps from every state they visited and pored over them as if preparing for semester finals.

"As if I don't have your testimony memorized," Brook responded to Niles' good-natured taunt. "You only have one of those."

"Remember when Les did that?" said Roger.

Roger Bosco did most of the driving. He loved being behind the wheel, and the Chrysler Town and Country Wagon in which they traveled happened to belong to his father. "I think it was one of our first engagements. Les introduced himself as Niles Jensen and quoted his testimony word for word. All Niles could do when it came his turn was to call himself Les Frank and do the same."

"I would have gotten away with it too," said Les. "But one of Niles' many girlfriends came to hear us and called me on it after the service. She said I'd never be half the man Niles was, and I immediately agreed."

"You'll have to explain that one for Ron," said Brook.

Brook Wilson chose to ride in the way-back, a third seat tucked in among all the luggage. He claimed it made it possible for him to read and study in peace, but it also meant he could sleep while they traveled. Too much reading made him carsick.

"I used to top the scale at almost three hundred pounds." Niles twisted around to face Ron in the seat behind him. "People never believed that I could sing tenor, so I decided my girth needed to match my vocal range. I've lost nearly one hundred pounds."

"Actually, we are pretty proud of Niles," Roger added. "It's not easy maintaining a consistent weight when traveling. You'll soon discover that church ladies are easily offended if you don't try all of their casseroles during dinner on the grounds."

Ron should have felt like the odd man out in the quartet as the new guy. But just two weeks into their schedule, comradery assured an acceptance as if they had traveled together for years. Each of the fellows had their peculiarities, but their dedication to Christ, and serving Him through music, melded them into a unit which functioned with few struggles.

In addition to collecting maps, Niles developed a fascination with historical roadside markers, insisting on stopping to read and photograph them any time they appeared. Some of the oldest signs marked Revolutionary War battlefields, while others alerted them to Underground Railroad sites, iron works, and Civil War locales. Pennsylvania alone had over 2,500 such signs, so the fellows made it a game to distract Niles when a sign might be approaching. He discovered kindred spirits on a stop in Little Rock, Arkansas. A family in one of the churches they visited shared how they spent every vacation visiting Civil War battlefields to discover what went wrong.

They developed a long list of how different military decisions might have changed the outcome of the war. Niles added one of their daughters to his growing list of pen pals.

The quartet watched the results of the 1980 Presidential election on a small, black-and-white television in a Motel Six in North Platte, Nebraska, on November 4. The landslide victory of Ronald Reagan over Jimmy Carter brought some satisfaction to Ron, but nothing like the news on Inauguration Day the next January when the announcement came that the Iranian hostages had been released. His dad had been right all along. Reagan would accomplish tasks which had proved impossible for his predecessor. A fleeting hope that the new President might hear of his ignominy and re-instate him in the FBI lasted no longer than the drive from Flagstaff to Phoenix.

Les Frank's fascination involved Major League Baseball stadiums. Since far fewer of those existed, the guys willingly arranged to visit any park near where they sang. They couldn't afford tickets to games, but Les developed a good collection of personal photographs in front of Camden Yards, Progressive Field, Wrigley, Dodger Stadium, and half a dozen others before their first year of travel ended.

The schedule that first year proved very similar to what they did for the college. Churches on Sunday morning and evening, midweek services on Wednesday or Thursday, and youth rallies on Saturday night. Sometimes the churches provided housing with member families. Stories of siblings who ran each other through the spin cycle of the clothes dryer, or bedrooms so full of greenery you could hardly find the bed provided entertainment on the next leg of their journey.

Sometimes they rented a motel room on their own when churches failed to provide housing. Free-will offerings ranged from a few dollars poured into their hands from an offering plate to a hundred dollar check they sent back to Helen to be banked. Enough gas money to arrive at their next destination sometimes took precedence over meals. A concert in Lead, South Dakota, attracted only twelve people, including a set of identical twin girls who explained that they were also performers and handed them tickets to their show at the Bloody Bucket Saloon later that evening. The unused tickets occupied a prominent position in the empty ashtray of the Chrysler.

By the beginning of their second year of travel, the Town and Country wagon approached the limit of its usefulness.

"We need a bus," Roger announced as they waited for a mechanic to replace the fuel pump on the Chrysler. "We can't keep pouring money into this heap of junk. Besides, a bus would solve our housing problems. Motel rooms are too expensive."

"I just happen to have a bus sitting in my front yard," joked Brook. "We can pick it up on our way through Charlotte."

They all laughed, but no one was laughing when they called Helen for an itinerary update that evening. Roger held the phone, relaying the message to the rest of them as she talked.

"Helen says she has turned our scheduling over to Mike Hitchcock at Nashville Gospel."

"Helen says what?" Niles nearly choked on the granola bar he had chosen for his supper, determined not to regain the weight he had lost.

"Helen has turned our scheduling over. . ."

"He heard you the first time," Les interrupted. "It was a rhetorical 'what.'"

Roger nodded and listened to Helen again. "Mike Hitchcock wants us to come to Nashville for a recording session. He heard us at the concert we gave in Chattanooga."

Les placed a hand over Nile's mouth to keep him from asking any more rhetorical 'whats,' and the four of them waited breathlessly for Roger's next message relay.

"Nashville Gospel wants to cut a demo, promote it to radio stations, and produce a record. They believe we have what it takes to go big-time."

Another long silence occurred as they watched Roger's mouth drop open at Helen's next words before repeating them.

"When we get to Nashville, they have a travel bus available for our use."

THE *CERTAIN SOUNDS'* CONTRACT with Nashville Gospel changed everything. Mike continued to schedule Sunday church services, but during the week they worked fairs, rodeos, conventions, and larger auditoriums, opening for groups like *The Speers, Wendy Bagwell and the Sunliters*, and the *Bill Gaither Trio*. People purchased tickets to hear them sing.

The bus turned out to be a 1971 Eagle Entertainer Coach with high mileage, onboard toilet, and six bunks. The fellows quickly made it their home.

By their third year of travel, they had become the headliners and others opened for them. Record sales removed the fear of not having enough gas money to make it to the next destination. Paying crowds made it possible to continue visits to churches on Sundays, something none of them wanted to give up. Music was not just a job. It was a ministry.

Niles continued to collect addresses for female pen pals as if they were Green Stamps. His first action at every church involved seeking out the pastor and checking to see if any letters awaited his arrival. The other fellows joked that he wrote to all the girls in duplicate or even triplicate, just changing the names and the addresses on his correspondence.

Roger met Les Frank's sister and started to save his dimes for weekly telephone conversations. Letters were also important, but hearing her voice took precedence. His focus in every town became the location of a phone booth. Les started calling him Superman, especially since his sister's name was Lois.

Brook and Les devised a ranking system from one to ten for the girls they met and spent hours on the road debating the relative value of redheads versus blondes, and whether sevens and eights were more approachable than tens. Les even claimed to have seen an eleven when they made a quick stop at the Grand Canyon. But no one else saw her, and he hadn't thought to take a picture.

Ron concentrated on his piano practice, using uprights, baby grands and even keyboards at every church they visited. Convinced that he had never even seen a girl who would qualify as a ten, much less an eleven, he remained friendly with all the young people they met, but uninterested in the complications of a long-distance relationship. It was hard enough to write to his mother once a week. Then came a stop in Elk Lodge, Montana.

CHAPTER SEVEN

BROOK AND LES WOULD have both given her a ten even though she was neither a blonde nor a ginger. Long, black braids hung almost to her waist. High cheekbones and dark irises revealed a classic Native American beauty. A simple, fringed leather vest and mid-length calico skirt distracted Ron from his prelude to the place where he made a very uncharacteristic mistake on a musical arrangement he had played hundreds of times. He felt as if she had stepped right out of the pages of *High, Wide, and Handsome*, the Montana history book his uncle James had sent him soon after the James Freeborn family moved to the Big Sky State.

"She's called Penny," his cousin Cynthia reported during their meal at the parsonage after the service. "I think it's short for Penelope or something like that. She's Arapaho, you know."

Ron didn't know. But he wanted to. He wanted to know everything he could possibly learn about Penny Whitman. She fascinated him in a fashion never previously encountered. Ten didn't qualify as nearly a high enough number to describe her. Lord Byron's "she walks in beauty like the night" came close, but even that description fell short. He longed to compose a sonata, or nocturne, or maybe a ballad in her honor. He wanted to rent Carnegie Hall and perform an entire concert with her as an audience of one.

"She'll be back tonight," said Cynthia. "Penny never misses a service here at the church. I'll introduce you."

"Introduce her to all of us," said Brook. "Except for Niles. He doesn't need one more addition to his little black book."

"I already have her address." Niles reached for another ear of sweet corn as the plate passed him.

"You do not," scoffed Les.

"Wouldn't put it past him," said Roger. "So, what is it, Romeo."

Niles finished chewing a row of sweet corn and followed that with a slow drink of water before answering. "Whitman Ranch, Elk Lodge, Montana."

James Freeborn's laugh echoed through the room. "Our postmaster might actually deliver that," he said when he had regained self-control. "Our city mayor actually had a letter delivered to him which was addressed to The Steamroller, Montana, and nothing else. He took great pride in the fact that they knew his reputation up in the main distribution center in Billings. But it's not the Whitman Ranch, it's Ab-Sa-Ro-Ka. Good guess, though. Most of the people you saw in church this morning live on ranches."

Niles shrugged. "At least I got Ron going. Never seen him interested in anyone's address before."

"She's a nationally ranked barrel racer." Cynthia helped her mother bring in a plate from the kitchen piled high with venison steaks. "I think she'll place first in the Calgary Stampede this year."

Les speared a thick steak off the top of the platter and tried to keep a straight face as he phrased his question. "Barrel racing? Can't be much competition in that unless the barrel is rolling downhill."

To the joy of the quartet members, Cynthia missed the smirk and started into a lengthy explanation. "The barrels don't race. Her horse runs a cloverleaf pattern around them, trying for the fastest time. Touching a barrel slows you down, and knocking one over deducts points. A five-second penalty really hurts when winners are determined by just thousands of a second. I can't believe you've never heard of barrel racing."

"He's pulling your leg, cuz." Ron speared his own steak and scowled at Les. "We've performed at more than one rodeo."

"Well then," Cynthia replied. "He'd better quit pulling my leg, or he may find out there's a foot attached to that leg which packs a pretty good kick."

"Cynthia," admonished her mother. "He's a guest."

"A guest who deserves a swift kick, Aunt Elizabeth." Ron defended his cousin. "After all this time on the road, we lost our guest status in any state about two years ago. Les deserves every come-back he receives."

"Besides," grinned Cynthia, "Dad's been pulling our legs ever since we were born. He used to tell us that we couldn't go to what he calls tourist traps because they let you get in free but charge you to get out. It was years before we realized he was talking about the souvenir shops they have at the end of each tour. You have to exit through the shop, and Will and I couldn't do that without begging for something. So, according to Dad, they charged us to get out."

"So, what does Sacajawea do when she's not chasing barrels?" Niles concentrated on carving up his meat, carefully avoiding eye contact with anyone. "Just asking on behalf of my friend Ron, of course. Since he wouldn't ask for himself. Since he's such a loner. Since all he wants to tickle are the ivories. Since. . ."

"Can it Niles. We get the point." Ron laughed.

"She and her father rent out cabins and do some guiding during hunting season. Her mother died not long after Penny was born. Lee does a wonderful job as a single dad." Pastor Freeborn fielded the question and then added his own coda, "Just answering on behalf of Ron, of course."

Mrs. Freeborn finally joined them at the table, which meant everything needed to be passed her way. None of the guys minded, with second helpings plentifully available.

"Penny also works as a ranger in Yellowstone Park during the summers. She leads trail rides." Cynthia poked Les in the ribs. "And no, they don't ride trails, they ride horses."

"That was going to be my next question," grinned Les, grabbing his side as if he had been gravely abused. "Does she offer private lessons to greenhorns? Just asking on behalf of my friend Ron, of course."

By the time the of the evening service, dozens of questions about Penny had been asked and answered, all on behalf of Ron.

He tried his best to concentrate on the keyboard before the service that evening. Even though he never missed a beat, he still knew exactly when she entered the room. He knew when Niles and Les finagled introductions through Cynthia. He knew when she took a seat in the front row on the piano side along with the Freeborns. And when the quartet had completed their portion of the evening program and he discovered that Cynthia had saved him a seat between her and Penny, he knew that someone special sat beside him, even though they had never exchanged anything more than a quick glance.

Penny's first words when the service concluded removed any lingering doubt that something truly noteworthy had occurred. As he completed the final chord progressions on his postlude, *O the Deep, Deep Love of Jesus*, a slim form joined him on the piano bench.

"In the style of J. S. Bach's *Jesu, Joy of Man's Desiring*," she said. "I'm Penny Whitman."

"Ron Freeborn," he said, the only reply he could manage. It was far too soon to say the rest of what raced through his mind. She knew the classics. He wanted to kiss her just for that fact alone. Her fascinating eyes had haunted him all afternoon. His desire to run his fingers down one of her braids reduced him to feeling like a junior high boy in the throes of his first crush. The only thing keeping him from fulfilling that desire was four sets of eyes watching him like hawks. Under each set of eyes, a mouth struggled to avoid a smirk. Brook and Les each held up ten fingers where only he could see them. Niles held up his little black book. Roger placed a hand in front of his mouth and whooped like an Indian. Silently, of course.

The next week flew by like a spring-storm-fed gully-washer rushing down a dry creek bed. Mike had booked three evenings at the Festival of Nations in Elk Lodge. The quartet repertoire included more than enough music to present three concerts without repetition. But the ethnic nature of the Festival prompted them to prepare some introductions and explanations which bridged the gap between their standard Southern Gospel and the Finnish, German, Mexican, and Native American heritage celebrated during the week. For Ron that bridge proved easy to cross. He played *Ein Feste Burg* for the Germans, Jean Sibelius' *Finlandia* for the Finns, and *Himno Nacional Mexicano* by Bocanegra for the Hispanics.

"I can play piano in any language," he told the appreciative audience before his performances.

The quartet had a harder time since they could only sing in English. Brook compensated for that by providing historical insight into the background of one of the crowd favorites, *How Great Thou Art*.

"Most of us associate this wonderful song with the voice of George Beverley Shea and the Billy Graham Evangelistic Crusades. Those words came to us from a British pastor, Stuart K. Hine, but that's not where the song began. Way back in 1886 a Swedish pastor by the name of Carl Boberg was caught in a violent thunderstorm. He heard the rolling thunder, and after the storm passed, he thrilled to the birds singing sweetly in the trees. Boberg wrote a poem with nine verses, and Swedish Christians began to sing it to the tune of an old Swedish folk song. The words were translated into German and then Russian before Hine heard them while serving as a missionary in Ukraine. He translated the Russian words into English and added a verse of his own. Shea made it a favorite in the Graham crusades. One hundred years after the original words were written, none other than Elvis Presley made the song famous again in its country of origin, Sweden."

Ron's arrangement for the quartet of the well-known song never failed to delight the audiences, whether their heritage included Swedish, German, Russian, or English ancestry. Every night as they came to the final chorus, hundreds of voices would join them, often singing in their native tongues.

"Then sings my soul my Savior God to Thee,

How great thou art, how great thou art."

During the days, Cynthia, Will, and Penny made it their goal to introduce the fellows to Big Sky Country. All eight of them crowded into

Penny's Land Cruiser and followed trails not much more than heavy ruts into the nearby Rocky Mountains. For exploration of even rougher terrain, they chose horseback. Winding single file up narrow paths, they watched the green meadows disappear and the pine ridges grow ever closer. Snow-capped peaks towered over them, seeming to grow taller the nearer they approached. Gossamer thin white clouds flirted with the rocky crags as if caught in a trap before breaking away and disappearing into the endless blue sky.

"We have always been a people of the land." Penny's love for the mountains and pride in her heritage prompted stories which fascinated the quartet. "We didn't worship the land as some have claimed. But we honored it and valued it. Our stories of creation, heroes, and tricksters provided insights into a spirit world which we recognized and tried to understand."

"Did you ever go on a vision quest?" Brook leaned back into the Jeep to avoid branches along the trail.

"No. That practice had just about disappeared before I became a teen. When I first heard the Christ-story, I immediately noticed the similarities between our traditional folktales and the biblical account. For example, the Navajo have many stores of a hero who enters unfamiliar territory and suffers in numerous ways, even to the place of death. A person with special powers comes to restore the hero. Since the entire human race descended from Adam and Eve, I began to see how those cultural myths had their roots in a common ancestry. Christ became my hero and I saw God as the one who rescued him from death."

"So, who is the trickster?" Roger poked Niles in the ribs. "Sounds like a good nickname for Les here."

Penny laughed. "The Trickster represented the desire of people not to be bound by rules and societal conventions. He delighted in sinning and getting away with it, even though that resulted in chaos. One story tells of a trickster in the form of a racoon who saw two blind men who had food provided daily by their tribe. When a meal consisting of eight pieces of meat was placed in front of them, the racoon stole four of the pieces. The men accused each other of taking more than their share, and the racoon slapped each of them on the face to rouse even more anger. Then the racoon stole the rest of the meal and ran away. From a distance he told them they needed to learn not to accuse each other so readily."

"But he got away with all their food," said Will. "That wasn't fair."

"For a trickster, fair only applies to what he can gain for himself. Those stories were shared with children in order to teach them not to be like him."

Ron divided his time between the awe-inspiring sight of the Rockies and the breath-taking beauty of their guide. She hadn't had an easy life, being raised by a single parent since her mother's death. She reminded him of the Mozart sonatas Helen had insisted on assigning during his piano lessons. The sonatas sounded dainty and cheerful but were fiendish to play. Like Mozart's music, he regarded their relationship as an improvisation. Every time he thought he figured her out according to classical conventions, he turned the page and discovered another hint of mischief. She fascinated him even more than the massive expanse of the Montana landscape their visit taught him to love. For the first time since they started on tour, he regretted the fact that they would be there only a week.

Uncle James joined them for a fishing expedition on the Red Rock River where he tried patiently to school them in the proper way to present a dry fly to rising trout. He also made sure that they took a drink from one of the clear mountain streams flowing into the Red Rock. "If you drink enough Montana creek water, you'll always come back," he promised.

On Thursday they got up before dawn and toured the southern loop of Yellowstone Park, with stops at Lower Geyser Basin to see the Paint Pots, Old Faithful, Yellowstone Lake, the Mud Volcano in Hayden Valley, and Inspiration Point at the falls of the Yellowstone. To Brook's delight they counted eleven elk, a moose, numerous deer, and a buffalo herd which brought them to a complete standstill as the huge, shaggy creatures shuffled across the highway. Penny pointed out a Grizzly bear with two cubs at the far end of a distant meadow.

"That's probably as close as you want to come to a Grizzly," she said. "Especially one with cubs."

Ron had never experienced a swifter passage of seven days. The final day of the Festival featured a rodeo. As he watched Penny circle the barrels dressed in a red and white flannel shirt, blue jeans, and red cowboy boots, his heart nearly stopped at the thought of leaving the next day. He knew from the time they had spent together that interest existed on her part as well. But she was west, and he was east. She was Levi's and he was Brooks Brothers. As much as he might be attracted, he could never justify taking her out of her Montana environment. She belonged in the mountains just like her Native American ancestors, and his future waited in Washington, D. C. The quartet traveled on, and he consoled himself with nothing more than an address.

Penny Whitman
Ab-Sa-Ro-Ka Ranch
Elk Lodge, Montana

CHAPTER EIGHT

THE BOMB EXPLODED AT exactly 10:58 p.m. on the evening of November 7, 1983. The north wing of the United States Capitol Building suffered approximately $250,000 in damages. Had the Senate not canceled a scheduled evening session, many would have died, despite the communique sent to a Washington radio station which read in part, "We did not choose to kill any of them this time."

"This time" was the part of the message which caught the attention of Deputy Director Judson Freeborn.

"I swear it's the same group we've been tracking for months," he said to his assistant Greg. "Their MO fits what we saw at Fort McNair and the Washington Navy Yard bombings. As far as I'm concerned, the Revolutionary Fighting Group, the Red Guerrilla Resistance, and this new Armed Resistance Unit are one and the same: the May 19th group, a bunch of women terrorists."

Switching off the Motorola radio when the news changed to an upbeat rendition of Michael Jackson's *Beat It*, Judson leaned back in his chair, staring out at the skyline of Washington, D.C. Darkness prevented any view of the Capitol Building, but he knew exactly what he would see when the sun rose the next morning. Smoke would still be rising from the building that represented the very best in world democracy. He knew this was only the most recent of several bombings of the historic structure. The most devastating had been when British troops burned both the Capitol and the White House in 1814. But that hadn't been on his watch. He had joined the fight soon after the 1971 bombing by the Weathermen, a radical faction of the Students for a Democratic Society.

The Bureau of Alcohol, Tobacco and Firearms, or ATF, had been established as an independent agency just ten years earlier, although their history dated back to the Revolutionary War. Their responsibility to enforce the provisions of Title XI of the Organized Crime Control Act placed them in the forefront of the investigation of the group calling themselves the Armed Resistance Unit.

"Reckon we better head over there and view the damage firsthand." Greg Levenson, Judson's assistant, downed the last of his third cup of coffee. He depended on the caffeine to keep him alert after joining his boss in the office at 3:00 a.m. "We have several sets of prints from the raid on 350 Omega Street after they broke Assata Shakur out of Clinton Correctional. Maybe we will get lucky."

But luck evaded Greg and Judson, as well as all the other government agencies involved in the investigation. One witness claimed to have seen a Middle Eastern-type male. Another one reported seeing an Hispanic man with a hooked nose. Capitol police remembered a white guy with a Puma sports bag walking into the building earlier in the day and emerging without the bag later that evening. No one said anything about suspicious women.

The bomb had been planted outside the Senate chamber. The explosion tore the door to Senator Robert Byrd's office completely off its hinges. Scraps from various paintings on the walls lay scattered throughout the hall. Daniel Webster's face in his portrait looked as if it had been ripped into tiny fragments by a grenade. Bricks, plaster, and glass littered the Republican cloakroom which had suffered a huge hole in its wall. Mirrors fractured. Chandeliers hung crookedly from the ceiling. Furniture resembled kindling. No evidence of a Puma bag remained in the debris.

"They must have had something against Webster," Greg joked as they observed the janitorial team already starting cleanup. "Daniel did prevent the Civil War for several decades through his compromises. Maybe that's their beef."

"They probably wished to destroy President Reagan instead of just Webster's portrait," said Judson. "The message to National Public Radio denounced his actions in Grenada and Lebanon. I expect they hate him far more than they do Webster. From my experience these domestic terrorists have little knowledge of history. All they know are their own grievances."

"Seems like a strange way to show hatred for the President. Why here instead of the White House?"

"This group will do anything to discredit Reagan. I'm surprised they haven't tried to rescue John Hinckley like they did Shakur. He's definitely one of their heroes even though his only motive was to impress that movie starlet."

"Maybe psychiatric facilities are more secure than prisons," joked Greg.

Satisfied that little evidence would be gained from the bomb site, the pair made their way back to ATF headquarters, hopeful that a lead would develop from some other direction. It was hard to believe that someone could walk into the Capitol of the most powerful nation in the world and leave a bomb without anyone noticing.

"Weren't you and Marilyn headed off to Falls Church tonight?" Greg asked.

"That was the plan. Ron's quartet will be singing. Expect she'll have to make the trip without me. Director Higgins is going to want all hands on deck for this investigation."

"That's a bummer. You haven't seen much of him the last few years."

"Goes with the territory. Just one of life's disappointments."

The plodding, often tedious, work which characterizes most of law enforcement paid off late that afternoon when a clerk from Master Hosts Inn on Bladensburg Road remembered a guest using the pay phone just outside the office a few minutes before 11:00 p.m. the previous night. His call proved to be the only solid lead out of all the tips which came pouring into the ATF office after a prime-time appeal for information.

"I like to watch people," he told Judson and Greg when they arrived at the motel. "These two were strange. For example, they both knew the number on the license plate of their car. One woman maybe. But two? Most people go out and look when I ask for the plate number, but these two just rattled it off like they had it memorized. And they both stood out there in the cold during the phone call. We have phones in the rooms. Why not use them? Strange. That's what I thought. They paid cash and insisted on getting a copy of the receipt immediately instead of waiting until they checked out the next day. Strange."

"May we see the register?" Greg reached for the logbook and turned it toward him though perfectly capable of reading it upside down.

"Absolutely." The clerk didn't hesitate, even knowing it violated company policy and he really should contact the manager. This was the most excitement he had seen since the Hell's Angels had roared in on their Harley Davidsons to protest the government regulations requiring the use of helmets.

"Terrible what happened over at the Capitol." He pointed at the logbook. "Ana Stackliff. That's the name right there. Doesn't mean it's real. We don't ask for identification beyond just the license plate. Room 144. One night. They were gone when I came to work this morning."

Anxious to see if his people-watching skills had succeeded, the clerk escorted them to the motel room and opened the door. "The maids have already cleaned. Need to have the room ready for the next guests you know. But you're welcome to look around." Instead of returning to the front desk, he continued to stand in the open door, watching as they checked out the room.

Even a cursory glance revealed the fact that Master Host maids worked efficiently. Greg stuck his head into the bathroom, lifted the duvet to look under the bed and pulled out all the dresser and desk drawers. He even rifled through pages of the Gideon Bible.

"Where do the maids dump the trash?" asked Judson after they had convinced themselves nothing in the room provided any leads.

"Laundry room. Could still be there. Let's go see." The eager clerk led them back toward the office and into an overheated room smelling of steam and soap. "They usually gather everything into one garbage bag before throwing it into the dumpster. That's it right there."

Banana peels. Candy wrappers. Half-eaten tacos. Bits of chips from the bottom of crumpled bags. Beer and soda cans. Newspapers and a paperback book. The detritus from a hundred travelers spread out over laundry tables.

"Sometimes police work stinks," laughed Greg as he gingerly removed a soiled diaper from the bag. Judson just groaned, but the clerk thought the remark hilarious.

"Might have something here." Judson spread out a crumpled receipt for Room 144 and then turned it over. "They've written on the back."

The words from the communique received and reported by NPR were written in flowing cursive. "We purposely aimed our attack at the institutions of imperialist rule rather than at individual members of the ruling class and government. We did not choose to kill any of them this time. But their lives are not sacred, and their hands are stained with the blood of millions."

At the bottom of the paper, another hand had written in large capital letters—MONTANA.

"Montana," said Greg. "Really? What would interest a gang of female terrorists in that state? It's huge, isn't it?"

"Only Texas and Alaska are larger. They call it Big Sky Country. My brother has been out there for several years trying to start a church. We better send word to the ATF office in Helena to keep their eyes peeled. Who knows what those crackpots might try next?"

CHAPTER NINE

CYNTHIA FREEBORN WANTED TO talk. That in itself was not unusual. Her father often said she had the spiritual gift of verbosity.

"You could talk a vulture off a fresh piece of carrion," he would say with a smile. The unusual came from the fact that Cynthia lacked anyone to talk to. Early spring in Montana meant calving and tilling. People didn't have time in the middle of the afternoon to visit the Elkhorn Café where she worked. Her only customer for the past half-hour had been the stranger in booth eleven.

She knew he was a stranger because of the Fiat parked out on Main Street. No one in Elk Lodge drove anything except pickups. At least, no self-respecting twenty-something drove anything else. Loafers instead of cowboy boots. Dockers instead of Levi's. Broad shoulders. Slightly shaggy hair. A quick smile but no casual wave of greeting which westerners offered even to those they met when driving. Definitely a stranger. Besides, she knew everyone in town. Elk Lodge wasn't that big.

"Howdy. More coffee?" Setting the coffee pot down on the table, Cynthia took the seat opposite the stranger. "Looking for anything in particular here in town? People often say Elk Lodge has to be a destination because it's the end of the road. Nowhere to go south of here except the Whitman place and the Continental Divide. One of the best rodeos in the state, but only during the Festival of Nations or on the Fourth of July. Good trout fishing in the Red Rock. Elk and deer in season. Unless you plan on poaching and you don't look like a poacher. Have to at least have a pickup for that. My name is Cynthia, but I guess you knew that. It's right here on my shirt pocket."

The stranger picked up the pot and refilled his own cup. "Hello, Cynthia. As a matter of fact, I am looking for something. A place to stay. More long-term than the motel I passed coming into town. Does anyone around here rent cabins or apartments?"

"Ab-Sa-Ro-Ka Ranch has cabins. I'm sure they would rent them year-round instead of just during hunting season. Want me to give Penny a call? Who should I say is looking?"

"Sorry. I should have introduced myself. Phil Adams." He stretched a long arm across the table and offered a handshake. "I need a place through the summer and perhaps early fall. That would be great if they have a cabin available."

"Well, it is a few miles south, but the road is good, and the only other long-term option would be back in West Yellowstone. Let me see what they have."

Jumping up from her chair, Cynthia stepped behind the counter and dialed. "Penny? Cynthia here. Say, I have this fellow here in the café looking for a place to settle down for a time. He's from. . ." Placing one hand over the receiver, she called back to where Phil sat in the booth. "Where did you say you were from?"

He grinned. She was better than an investigative reporter. "Washington," he called back. "Washington, D.C."

"He's from Washington, not the state. Back east. Plans to stay for the summer and maybe on into fall."

She smiled as she listened to the response from the other end of the line and then resumed her seat across from the man, no longer a stranger. No one stayed a stranger for long in Montana. At least not when Cynthia was around.

"You're in luck. Penny says you can have your choice. They're all open and available. Shouldn't have to worry about getting through the snow this time of year, although we've been known to get a few inches early in May. Head south on Main Street, cross the bridge over the Red Rock River, and there's no other road except the one that leads to the ranch. About seven miles and you'll be there. Penny said she would watch for you."

"Much obliged. Does the mayor pay you to promote Elk Lodge or is that a volunteer position?"

Cynthia laughed. "Have you heard of Will Rogers? My dad says I'm just like him. Not that I am Cherokee like he was, but because of his famous saying, 'I never met a man I didn't like.'"

"Cherokee?"

"Cherokee Nation. Indian Territory down in Oklahoma. Dad reminds me often of another one of Roger's quotes that I tend to forget. 'Never miss a good chance to shut up.' I'd better quit jabbering and let you get on down the road."

"Not at all. I don't mind. I would love to hear more about this part of the country. Are there many Cherokee Indians around?"

"Not in Montana. Blackfeet, Crow, Chippewa, Salish, and Cheyenne mostly. Lee Whitman is Arapaho. He married an Irish lass, so Penny is half Irish. But she still thinks of herself as Native American. They moved here from the Dakotas. But you don't need to worry. None of them are on the warpath anymore. We like to tease our eastern cousins when they come to visit, but Custer's Last Stand happened over a hundred years ago."

"So, you have relatives back east?" Phil sipped slowly at his coffee. Learning about a new location had never been this easy before. Westerners apparently had nothing to hide.

"In Washington, in fact. My uncle works for the Bureau of Alcohol, Tobacco and Firearms. I know it's a big place. I'm sure you've never heard of him. Do you work for the government too?"

"As a matter of fact, I do. But not ATF. I'm with the EPA, the Environmental Protection Agency."

He offered the blatant lie without so much as a flinch. What hick from outer Montana would ever know the difference? They lived so far from civilization that he hadn't even seen a Walmart for days. He drove on a two-lane interstate highway to get there. A two-lane interstate. Unbelievable.

"What about your father? Is he government as well?" Phil took another sip of coffee.

"Nope. Dad is a pastor. We moved to Montana about five years ago to start a church here in Elk Lodge. We meet in the basement of the library. You'll have to come some time. He's a great preacher."

"I'd love to," Phil lied again. Religion he could do without. "I will definitely plan on that. I guess it won't be too hard to find the library. In fact, I think I drove right past it on my way into town. If he's anything like you, I imagine everyone in town knows him as well. What did you say was his name?"

"Freeborn. James Freeborn. I'll tell him to watch for you."

"You do that." He drained the last of his coffee and placed a dollar on the table for his drink and a tip. "And thanks for making the arrangements with the Whitmans. I expect I'll be seeing you around."

Cynthia grabbed the cup and saucer in one hand and wiped down the table with the other. "Good to meet you, Phil. Welcome to Montana."

CHAPTER TEN

BACKSTAGE AT RYMAN AUDITORIUM resembled the chaotic assembly of ropes, flats, and teasers they had seen at hundreds of similar stages all across America. But this was not just any stage. This was Nashville. The scene of the National Quartet Convention. Ron Freeborn and the quartet watched in awe as members of the Kingsmen, Talleys, and Cathedrals paraded past. Ron nearly swallowed his tongue when Mr. Piano, Whitey Gleason, who played for the Blackwood Brothers, offered him a high five.

"You'll do well kid," Gleason growled. "Just pretend you're back in the Chugwater Chapel in Skunk Holler, Tennessee. We've all been there."

They had been there. The old Geoff Mack favorite *I've Been Everywhere* could have been written to describe their travels over the past five years.

And now they were in Nashville. At the Saturday night show. Waiting for an introduction from Master of Ceremonies Wendy Bagwell. He could see the gleaming, twelve-foot, Bosendorfer Grand he would be playing while the quartet sang. Four years since they struck out on their own. Four years to make the finals of the National Talent Search Competition with a chance to win six hours of recording time, three hours of mixdown time, five hundred albums pressed, besides this spot on the Saturday night show of the National Quartet Convention.

The Cathedrals kicked off the evening featuring their award-winning bass George Younce on *Step into the Water*. The capacity crowd cheered and hollered and clapped along as the Dixie Melody Boys, Speer Family, Hoppers, Gold City, and the Talleys entered the spotlight.

When Wendy Bagwell called for the Certain Sounds, Ron took a deep breath and followed the fellows out onto the stage, waving to the audience as they took their places in front of the mic stands.

"Niles Jenson, tenor. Les Frank, second tenor. Roger Bosco, baritone. Brook Wilson, bass, and Ron Freeborn, accompanist," said Bagwell over the top of the welcoming applause.

Taking Whitey Gleason's advice, Ron attacked the Bosendorfer as if it were an old upright in the Chugwater Chapel. His fingers raced across the keyboard as they had countless times before, introducing Joel Hemphill's *He's Still Working on Me*. By the time the quartet had sung the first words, all fear of the audience disappeared, and it was just the five of them making music as they had countless times before. The enthusiastic response from the crowd carried them into his own arrangement of *I'll Fly Away*. The "hallelujahs" in the chorus prompted hundreds of "hallelujahs" in response from the crowd.

When the last notes of Nile's high tenor voice had flown away, the announcement of the National Talent Search Competition proved almost anti-climactic. The entire audience rose to its feet, cheering, shouting, and applauding as the Certain Sounds accepted their trophy.

"And now," came Bagwell's voice over the microphone. "Let me introduce the winner of the Best Individual Performer for 1984."

Offering a dramatic flourish in the direction of the Bosendorfer, and pausing for effect, the words were almost obscured by the shouts of anticipation and appreciation from the audience.

"Ron Freeborn," he shouted.

Helen Forrester watched with pride as Ron gave a quick bow and then sat down again in front of the keyboard. People started to applaud as he played the first measures of a song they all knew as a result of the thousands of AWANA clubs spread across the nation, *The Assurance March*. She hardly recognized it as the same tune he had played in his fourth-grade recital. Key changes, cadenzas, and flourishes transformed it into a personal *tour de force* for her former student. Silence settled over the multitude as he played the same notes in the classical style of Johann Sebastian Bach. Next came a German waltz variety as he enthralled them with his totally new arrangement of the *Assurance March Around the World*. The waltz segued into Jamaican calypso, a Chinese version in perfect fifths, a Hawaiian luau, an Egyptian folk music rendition, a Jewish mesh with *Hava Nagila,* and finally a southern gospel style which had everyone on their feet once again, clapping in rhythm.

The applause continued through multiple attempts by Ron and the quartet to leave the stage, until finally they were back once more in the Green Room.

"How do you think we really did?" Out of the spotlight, the adrenaline flowed strong. Roger collapsed into a chair while Niles and Les kept punching each other's shoulders. "We know how Ron did, though I have no idea where he came up with that arrangement and even kept it from the four of us. But National Talent Search winners? Is it really true? Wow."

Brook answered Roger's question with a sly smile. "How did we do? The bass rocked but the baritone could have been stronger."

"Wasn't asking you," Roger grinned. "What did you think, Ron?"

"I think the Certain Sounds just wowed the audience at the National Quartet Convention. You fellows did great. Just wish we could keep traveling."

Even before the announcement had been made, Ron knew that the quartet would be awarded the trophy as winners of the National Talent Search Competition. Helen had been in the audience all week and assured him that no other group even began to measure up to the Certain Sounds. Besides that, she was convinced he would be earning the coveted title of Best Individual Performer. Several of the judges, men she had known for years, suggested to her that he be ready for a premiere performance when the award announcement happened. Now, for the second time in his life, the prospect of success seemed destined for disappointment. Not that the awards themselves disappointed. The honor for the quartet and his own accomplishments held tremendous personal value. The disappointment stemmed from the fact that nothing further would result from four years of effort. First, the abrupt ending to his FBI training, and now the break-up of the quartet. For the second time in his life, he felt a strong kinship with Jeremiah when he wrote his Lamentations. "I am the man who has seen affliction by the rod of His wrath. He has led me and made me walk in darkness and not in light."

"We could keep traveling if Roger would give up his wedding plans." Les quit punching Niles and started shadow boxing in front of Roger instead. "I never should have introduced him to my sister. Maybe I can still convince her to give him the old heave-ho."

"Too late for that. I've already rented tuxedos for all of you." Roger leaned back in the chair to avoid the wild swings. "Two more weeks and I'll be an old married man. I have to settle down and get a job. Do you realize we traveled for four years and not one of us has a savings account?"

"It's been a great run," agreed Brook. "But not really profitable. Just seems wrong to leave it at the top of our game. We could start pulling in the big bucks now."

"I feel the same way, Les," added Niles. What are we going to do with those five hundred albums we won?"

"Divide them five ways and live off the profits for the next thirty days," joked Brook. "I'd like to keep the group together as well, but Roger's not the only one who has plans. I've been asked to hold a week of revival meetings. Billy Sunday, Billy Graham, Brook Wilson. You can all say you knew me when."

"When we knew you, all you did was sing bass and repeat the same two sermons *ad infinitum*," teased Les. "Where's the meeting? New York City? Los Angeles? Chicago?"

"Elk Lodge, Montana. Remember when we sang there for Ron's uncle? He's invited me to come back and preach for a week."

"That means you'll have to write five more sermons. Won't be able to just keep repeating the two of them you use now." Niles dropped into a chair but kept his shoulders moving. The guys often teased him that he never stopped moving. He would take a nap in the bus and be bumping his head constantly against the back of the seat while sound asleep.

"You could take us along to give the illustrations." Les grabbed Niles by the shoulders and tried to stop his movement, but instead they both shook together. "I can tell the story of the chilblained eagle freezing to the ice and going over Niagara Falls better than you can. He dug his fingers into Niles' shoulders and lowered his voice in imitation of Brook's bass.

"The eagle heard the rush of the falls but wouldn't surrender his fatal grasp on the carcass. His talons dug into the ice, freezing in place as he tore piece after piece off the carrion until, spreading his wings to avoid certain death, he found himself frozen fast to the swirling ice floe. With a screech of terror, he plunged over the falls to certain death."

"Pitch perfect," laughed Roger. "Couldn't have done it better myself."

Brook joined in the laughter, knowing the fellows had all his sermons memorized and not just the illustrations. "Be glad to take you along. In fact, Pastor Freeborn suggested as much. What do you think? Shall we take a reunion tour to Montana before calling it quits?"

Les shook his head. "Dad has asked me to start working in the furniture store. He thinks he wants me to take over the business. On the road again won't work for me."

"Same here," said Niles. "Graduate school classes start the week after the wedding. Back to school for me."

"Ron? You headed back to D.C.?"

"Right. I renewed my application to the Academy. Maybe it will happen now that there's a Republican administration. But nothing moves fast in Washington. I could manage a week or two in Montana. Just don't plan on me giving any illustrations or sermons. I'll stay at the piano and let you do the talking."

Except to Penny, he told himself. I'll do my own talking to her.

"Great," said Brook. "That's settled then. You can be my Homer Rodeheaver. Montana here we come!"

CHAPTER ELEVEN

THE LIBRARY IN ELK Lodge, Montana, originated with a grant from Andrew Carnegie in 1917. Citizens chose a Classical Revival style for the stone building which dominated the entrance to town. It occupied a triangular-shaped lot where Main Street and Lincoln Avenue split. A formal arched entryway stood at the top of a staircase, said to symbolize the fact that people were elevated by learning. A lamppost at the foot of the stairs had a similar function as a symbol of enlightenment.

Cynthia often speculated that the librarian, Frances Fenton, had been there since the building first opened its doors. Frances introduced her to the Bobbsey Twins and Nancy Drew when she was younger, and more recently to Zane Grey and Louis L'amour.

"Let me help you with that, Miss Fenton." Cynthia grabbed one end of a large box the librarian lugged up the staircase. "More books?"

"It would take more than the two of us to carry a box of books this large. I do appreciate the help. I shouldn't have tried it on my own. But I am so excited I couldn't wait. The Montana Library Association sent us our own computer. A TRS80. I'm not sure what that means, but they're going to send Ethel Planck down to connect us to the library in Helena. They tell me that one day soon every library in the state will be connected through something called the World Wide Web. We'll be able to loan books from anywhere in the state and not just from our own collection."

"I can see why you are excited." Cynthia balanced one corner of the box with her left hand while pulling open the door to the library. "Where shall we put it?"

"On that table behind the circulation desk, I guess. I don't expect anyone else will know how to use it, and I won't have any idea until the training. What can I do for you this morning?"

"Just thought I would run downstairs and make sure things are ready for church tomorrow if that's all right."

"Any time. I expect your father is getting excited about the revival meetings he's been announcing. Some young fellow who was here last year with the quartet, right?"

"Brook Wilson. But that's not all. My cousin Ron is coming too. He's the one who plays the piano like Rudy Atwood from The Old-Fashioned Revival Hour. They should be arriving sometime this week."

"That should make Penny happy." Miss Fenton took a letter opener from the drawer of her desk and began to cut the tape on the box. Cynthia grinned. "Miss Fenton, are you playing matchmaker?"

The librarian looked puzzled and then smiled in return. "Not at all. I just know how much Penny dislikes having to play for the church services. That's all. She'd much rather ride a saddle than a piano bench."

"Well, I for one would love to see her and Cousin Ron get together. I think they would match perfectly."

Miss Fenton opened the Radio Shack box and lifted out the square-shaped, white plastic contraption which featured a small monitor with an attached keyboard. "They said all we needed to do was plug it in," she muttered, "but what if I mess something up? Maybe we should wait until they send Ethel to help."

"It can't be that hard. Looks like a typewriter with a television hooked on. Let's plug it in and see what happens."

Cynthia unwound the power cord and crawled under the table to locate an outlet. Inserting the plug into the wall, she stood back up and stared at the equipment on the table, but nothing happened.

"Maybe we should read the instructions."

Miss Fenton pulled a booklet from the box and laid it on the table. "Introduction to your Disk System, TRS-80 Model 4," she read.

"It says it can be used for business, education, personal finance, programming, and entertainment," added Cynthia. "I wonder what kind of entertainment?"

"I guess we'll have to find out. Here we go. I'll read, and you follow the directions. How to set up the Model 4."

For the next hour the two of them perused the manual, learning about random access memory and read-only memory, BASIC programming language and DOS operating systems. By the time they arrived at page thirty-nine and the words "Applications for the Model 4 are limited only by the imagination," Cynthia was ready to insert a floppy disk and start typing, but not Miss Fenton.

"There's just too much to learn. We can't possibly do this without help. I'll just wait until Ethel comes from the Library Association. We've lived this long without computers, I guess we can wait another week or two."

Cynthia tried unsuccessfully to hide her disappointment. "I have an idea. That new fellow from the EPA who is staying out at Whitmans. I bet he knows something about computers. Maybe we could ask him. He's from back east. You know what they say, everything starts on the east coast, jumps to California and eventually makes it back to the Midwest."

"I don't want to be a bother."

"It won't be," urged Cynthia. "Let me see if he would be willing to help. I bet he'd be glad to take a look at your new computer."

"All right. Go ahead and talk to him. In the meantime, I had better get busy updating the card catalog. That's something no new-fangled computer is ever going to replace. You can be sure of that."

CHAPTER TWELVE

"THEY'RE HERE," SHOUTED WILL, shoving his chair back from the table and racing to the front door. "They're here."

The sound of a vehicle in desperate need of a new muffler alerted the Freeborn family to the arrival of their expected guests. Cynthia and her folks quickly joined Will in the front yard as Ron and Brook climbed wearily from the van.

"Do you have any idea how far you live from civilization?" Ron greeted Will with a high five, offered brief hugs to his aunt and cousin, and shook hands with his uncle. "You all remember Brook Wilson here, right? He's been grousing about the lack of any McDonalds since we left Denver."

"You're just in time for supper." Mrs. Freeborn invited them into the house and set out two more plates. "It's not McDonalds, but it's free."

"Thanks, Aunt Elizabeth. I could eat a bear."

"Good thing," grinned James, "because that's what we're having."

Brook looked at the plate of meat sitting on the table. His eyes grew wide. "Really? Is that bear? I didn't know you were allowed to kill them."

"You're thinking about grizzly bears," said Will. "They're endangered. But not the black and brown ones. You just need to be sure you're not in Yellowstone Park when you shoot them. They are protected there."

"So, you really kill them and eat them?" In spite of his hunger, Brook set down his knife and fork, not sure his stomach could handle bear steak.

"Welcome to Montana, Brook," laughed Ron. "You're in the wild west now. But I have a feeling this is one of my uncle's jokes, right Uncle James?"

Pastor Freeborn laughed. "It's bare meat all right. No hair on it at all. Actually, this is elk steak. Some of the best meat you'll ever eat. We're sure glad you got here in time to share it. Let's pray and dig in."

Mashed potatoes, fresh corn on the cob, fruit salad, and large glasses of iced tea joined the "bare" meat as they enjoyed the abundance of the wild west. Elizabeth wanted to know all about the wedding, and Cynthia was curious about the quartet convention.

"First place," said Brook. "Not bad for our first attempt at the Talent Search Competition. Some of those groups have been competing for years. No recording contract though, which is just as well since Roger chose to abandon us."

"Disappointments are often His appointments." Elizabeth brought a platter of brownies from the kitchen and handed them to Brook. "Cynthia made these, so I know Will won't touch them, but the rest of us can enjoy them."

Ron joined in the fun by lifting the platter high over Will's head as he passed it to Cynthia. "All the more for us, cuz."

When the brownies got back to the head of the table, James placed one carefully in the center of his son's plate. "I insist, Will. Wouldn't want you to offend your sister by refusing one of her delicious desserts. Buck up and eat it like a man."

"If I have to," grinned Will, attacking the brownie with his fork. "I suppose I must. Have to keep peace in the family."

"We've made arrangements for the two of you to bunk out at Ab-Sa-Ro-Ka. Lee's hunting cabins are quite comfortable even though they aren't heated. Shouldn't need a fire this time of year anyway." Pastor Freeborn passed the brownies around again, and this time no one skipped over Will, who obviously enjoyed his sister's dessert. "We've announced the meetings for the same week as the rodeo since folks will be coming into town for that already. The Fourth falls on a Wednesday, so we'll hold services three days before and two days after. Not sure yet what to do on Saturday. Maybe a youth rally. That gives us a week to canvas the town with flyers."

"And a week for Brook to work up a couple more sermons. He only needed two when we were out on the road," teased Ron.

"I've been working on that." Brook cut off another piece of elk steak. "I'll be ready."

Cynthia helped her mother clear the table and carry the dishes into the kitchen, even though it was Will's turn to wash. "Penny and Phil want to go on a trail ride tomorrow. Would that be ok, Dad?"

"Fine with me. It was good to see Phil in church yesterday. Seems like a nice young man."

Hurriedly swallowing his bite of meat, Brook asked the question he knew Ron was anxious to voice. "Phil? Phil who? Is that someone we met last time we were here? Just asking on behalf of Ron, you know."

Cynthia and Will laughed as their cousin glared at Brook.

"He's here on business for the Environment Protection Agency," said Cynthia. "Something about oil exploration. He's renting a cabin out at Whitmans too, so you'll be neighbors."

"Whitman," continued Brook. "That name sounds familiar. Didn't they have a daughter named Nickel, or something? Just asking on behalf of Ron. Wasn't she a barrel racer or something? Not a very fair race, barrels don't even have legs."

"You guys tried that one last time, silly," said Cynthia. "It's Penny, not Nickel. She's going to win at our local rodeo this year and qualify to compete in the Helena Stampede. She's already nationally ranked, so that will qualify her for Nationals. Are you ready to head out to the ranch? Dad said I could take the Jeep and show you the way. You can't get lost between here and there, but that way I can introduce you to Penny and her father, and maybe Phil."

James nodded agreement. "We are glad you're here, Brook. And glad you brought Ron along, too. Cynthia, why don't you leave the Jeep out at the ranch and bring the van back. I'll arrange to have the muffler replaced while you head off into the mountains for your trail ride tomorrow. You fellows will scare off all the wild game in the entire county if we don't do something about that noise. Wouldn't want Brook to miss seeing a bear or two while you are here just because of a noisy muffler."

Brook wasn't sure how to respond to the possibility of encountering a bear in the wild, but Will helped him out with a call from the kitchen. "Don't mind Dad, Brook. The guys in our Boy's Brigade tell him the only time they believe him is when he is in the pulpit. The bears know to stay in the park where they are safe."

"And that's where we're going on the trail ride tomorrow," added Cynthia. "Right into Yellowstone National Park."

CHAPTER THIRTEEN

"This may be my favorite spot in the entire world." Penny Whitman reined in her palomino at the top of a rise overlooking the Red Rock River at the very place where it exited Yellowstone National Park.

Ron watched as she swung a leg easily over the horse and dropped gracefully to the ground. His cousin Cynthia did the same. He wasn't sure he could even lift his leg, much less stand on it when he dismounted. They had been riding for about an hour since Cynthia joined them at the Whitman Ranch. His legs felt like they had been riding for days. At least Brook and Phil were also dismounting cautiously, trying not to show the effects of a long time spent in the saddle.

"Just drop the reins on the ground, guys." Penny patted the neck of her horse. "They won't go anywhere."

Cottonwoods greeted the early summer weather with blossoms that looked like popcorn popping from every branch. The meadow sported an artist's palette of colors. Indian paintbrush, Lewis monkeyflower, and arnica. A bull elk grazed contentedly, paying little attention to the two cows nearby. Cascades of water rushing over the rocks provided musical accompaniment to the beauty of the Montana landscape before spreading slowly across the meadow. The peaks of the still snowcapped mountains lay inverted on top of the watery mirror.

"Are we in Yellowstone yet?" asked Phil.

"That tall ridge in the distance marks the boundary of the park. That is the closest the caldera comes to the edge of the park in any direction. Cross that ridge and you can see Lower Geyser Basin just to the west of Old Faithful."

"Wow," said Brook. "Can we go there?"

"Not today. But we'll definitely make another trip into the park while you are here. We only managed the south loop last time. It will be a lot easier to drive in through West Yellowstone rather than following this trail further. This is pretty rough terrain here along the Continental Divide."

"Didn't we cross a road back a way?" Ron dropped the reins of the bay Penny had chosen for him, thankful for the gentle, lazy manner in which the horse responded. He wasn't sure he could have handled the black gelding his cousin rode as if she had been born in the saddle. Both of the girls demonstrated excellent horsemanship. They rode tall in the saddle with an ease that made riding seem effortless. He admired the picture they presented framed against the backdrop of the Rocky Mountains. Wrangler jeans and flannel shirts fit them comfortably, unlike the stiff new denim he and the other fellows wore. He thought it would probably take at least a year of riding before his western wear truly felt comfortable.

"An old logging trail," said Penny. "You can hardly call it a road. It leads to an abandoned gold mine called the Fairweather. Historians claim it was discovered by the same William Fairweather who struck it rich in Alder Gulch. But it never came close to producing the thirty million in gold they took out of Virginia City. We can stop and take a look on our way back if you want."

"That would be great," said Phil, still holding onto the reins of his mount as if afraid the horse would bolt if he let loose.

"Actually, it's probably fortunate that the mine wasn't prosperous," said Cynthia. "This valley would look a whole lot different if a gold rush had arrived. The population of the fourteen miles around Virginia City exploded to over 10,000 people in just the first three months." The young girl turned around to look at Phil. "Is that why the EPA is interested in this part of the country? They don't think people are going to start moving here, do they?"

"Not for gold," said Phil. "Oil. The Secretary of the Interior espouses this crazy idea that federal property should be available for oil exploration because of world shortages. Instead of working for peace in the Middle East, he wants to destroy the peace of this pristine national treasure. Even though he resigned last fall, there are still those who think it's a good idea. I'm here to make certain that doesn't happen."

"They'll never allow drilling in the park," remarked Penny. "It has been protected from development for over a hundred years now. Besides, disturbing the groundwater could have disastrous effects."

Cynthia helped Penny pull lunch from the saddlebags and pass sandwiches around to the fellows. "I did a science report on the caldera last year. Did you know that some scientists think we are due for another supervolcano explosion? The Yellowstone caldera covers an area of the park forty-five miles from side to side and thirty miles long. Can you imagine the destruction which would result from an explosion that size?"

"And you think that drilling could trigger an eruption?" Brook accepted the sandwich and found a rock to sit on.

Cynthia sat down beside him. "No, but it could change the park in other ways. Norris Geyser basin has been changing daily for more than ten years. An area of land larger than Chicago started breathing."

"Is this another one of the famous Freeborn jokes?" laughed Ron. "You're as bad as Uncle James. Since when does the earth start breathing."

"Not a joke, cousin," she protested. "That's the way they describe it. There's a huge body of magma under Norris basin. Magma bubbles out and escapes from about a mile below the surface, and the land sinks. Then it gets stuck, and the pressure builds up so the entire area rises by several inches. It's like the land is breathing in and out."

"She's right," added Penny. "Steamboat Geyser, much larger than Old Faithful, has been erupting at a record-breaking pace for the last two years. Since all the geysers are connected by means of underground tunnels, drilling in one area would affect every other paint pot, geyser, and hot pool in the entire region."

"Which is exactly why it must not happen." Phil grew excited about the support from the girls. "Oil drilling would totally destroy this national treasure. Look what happened to the area around Butte when the Anaconda Copper Company started their open pit mining. Greed scarred the earth in ways from which it will never recover. Reagan wants to do the same here, just like he did in Alaska."

"Like Reagan did in Alaska?" questioned Ron. "The President signed the Alaska National Interest Lands Conservation Act back in 1980. The Arctic National Wildlife Refuge is the largest protected wilderness in the United States. How can you compare that to the Anaconda company?"

"Sure. That's what the administration says," sneered Phil. "But that same bill deferred the decision on oil drilling in one of the coastal areas. One and a half million acres are still open for exploration even though they closed the rest. Now Reagan wants to do the same thing here. As far as I'm concerned, we shouldn't be drilling at all, anywhere. We're here to protect Mother Earth, not exploit her."

"It certainly would be a shame to see oil wells spoiling this pristine view," agreed Penny.

"So, you think we should scrap all the gas-guzzling automobiles and go back to original horsepower?" Ron wasn't sure why he felt it necessary to argue with Phil. He hated the idea of anything spoiling the scene in front of them as well. But something about Phil's attitude irritated him. Maybe it was the way he treated Cynthia. She was far too young to be interested in a twenty-something. Maybe it stemmed from the way he looked at Penny.

Was he simply jealous? In any case, he wasn't about to swallow the extreme environmentalism Phil seemed to favor. "It is possible to develop natural resources without destroying the earth, you know."

"We've been doing that for years here in Montana," agreed Penny. We appreciate the land and try to preserve it."

"That's because you're a Native," argued Phil. "As far as I'm concerned, the entire west should still belong to your people. All those broken promises and covenants with the Native population is one of the blackest marks on American history."

"But we're not the ones who broke those promises," said Cynthia. "We don't treat the Native Americans as second-class citizens. When Penny went to Girl's State, they elected her as governor. And I wouldn't be at all surprised to see her serving in that office in Helena before too many years have passed. People are already after her to run. You only have to be twenty-five to serve as governor in Montana."

"Governor? Really?" asked Brook. "Why would you want to do that, Penny?"

"I'm not sure that I want to at all. It's people like Cynthia and my good friend Alicia Walks-Softly who are pushing me toward politics. But I do have a real desire to see life improve for my people. Life on the reservations has not been easy for them."

"So why are they still forced to live on reservations like cattle?" Phil glared at Ron as he asked the question, recognizing him as the greatest antagonist.

Penny watched the interchange between the two and tried to disarm the tension. "Do we live on a reservation, Phil? Dad owns one of the largest ranches in the entire state. I want to help my people see that they can do more for themselves, instead of depending on the government."

"Your dad is the exception that proves the rule," argued Phil. "We studied all about this in class at Columbia. White people have dominated the culture here in America ever since Plymouth Rock. Superior weapons, systematic genocide, and racial injustice."

"Wow. That's heavy." Brook grabbed another sandwich from the plate on the blanket. "I need more sustenance just to even think about all of that. But I will say this. If we need to go back to just riding horses, I'm going to need some more lessons. There's no way I could ever ride a horse all the way back to Ohio."

Penny laughed. "You've been doing great, fellows. I've led some trail rides where greenhorns begged to turn around after the first ten minutes. We'll make sure we stop several times on the way back to the ranch. In fact, the mine is only about fifteen minutes away so that can be our first rest area."

The Fairweather mine entrance consisted of little more than two rough-cut boards with a crudely fashioned mantle. Cut right into a rock face, it stared at them like an empty tomb. Tumbleweeds caught on the boulders had dried in place, nearly obscuring the opening.

"Doesn't look like much now," said Penny. "But Fairweather is said to have followed a vein for almost a mile into the mountain before it petered out. The problem was that they didn't take time to shore up the ceiling. It's not safe at all. They finally abandoned it when water started to seep in, and they thought they might have gotten close to one of the geysers."

"What did they do with the gold?" asked Ron.

"It still had to be separated from the rock. They couldn't see enough reason to bring in heavy sluice boxes. Besides, they were too far from the river. So, they carried it down to Red Rock, crushed it by hand and used gold pans. Turned out to be too little profit for the effort it took, especially when Alder Gulch proved so lucrative."

"Do you think there's any gold left?" Brook kicked at some of the stones near the entrance to the tunnel.

"Pick up some of those stones you are kicking around, and we'll see. I can show you how to pan for gold. We might even find a few flakes. After all, this is Montana. *Oro y Plata, Gold and Silver* has been the motto since territory days. If you can't strike it rich in Montana, you can at least give it a try."

CHAPTER FOURTEEN

JUDSON AND GREG ARRIVED on the scene within minutes after receiving a report of the bombing of the South African Embassy.

"We bombed the South African Embassy in solidarity with resistance to South African human rights violations. Down with apartheid. Victory to the Freedom Fighters. Defeat U.S. Imperialism. Guerrilla Resistance." The message sent to various media outlets followed up the now familiar warning call to the Embassy telling everyone to evacuate the building or lives would be lost.

Judson knew the attack reflected negatively on ATF because of an earlier robbery of a Stop and Shop where the perpetrators posed as agents from the Drug Enforcement Administration. Flashing what looked like U.S. Government IDs, they had executed Form Ao 93, claiming cocaine and marijuana were being sold in the store. The two would-be agents gained access with their fake badges and then used pistols to force the manager to open the safe.

"I expect that money made possible the purchase of the materials for the bomb at the Embassy," mused Judson as they inspected the damage. "Five bombings in twenty months. Something has to be done."

"Still think it might be the Weather Underground?" Greg nursed his cup of coffee, not sure when they would have time to stop for a refill.

"Not likely. The Underground is practically defunct. It must be the May 19th group. We'll have a better idea when we analyze the physical evidence. So far each bomb site has yielded similar fragments."

"It's not like they are trying to hide their involvement. The communiques sound nearly identical. The U.S.A. stands guilty of racism toward Black and Latino peoples. Ronald Reagan should be impeached. Israel and South Africa dominate Palestinian and South African freedom fighters economically, politically, and militarily. And the U.S. leads the corrupt imperialists of the world."

"That about sums it up. I think they would stop at nothing to defeat Reagan in the election this fall." Judson stooped to pick up what looked like a scrap of metal used in the bomb construction.

"Defeat Reagan. Destroy Israel. Defame the Moral Majority. You would think they could find at least one thing they like about our country."

"They're just a bunch of thugs, like President Nixon said. The only difference with the May 19th group is that they are all women thugs. You certainly can't call them ladies."

"Maybe we'll get a break this time. Say, how is your son's application to the Academy going this time? Will he be joining us soon?" Greg set down his coffee cup and started picking through the litter for more clues.

"I think it's going much better. At least Reagan's appointees aren't delaying it like Carter's did."

"That had to be one of the most devious plans I've seen in Washington, to deny Ron a place in the Academy because you had the courage to oppose Carter's waffling on the Iran hostage situation."

"Typical politics, I guess," shrugged Judson. "No one would ever admit he interfered, but the application got rejected the same day I was interviewed, and suggested it was time for the President to get up off his Oval Office chair and take some action. I know it was a great disappointment to Ron, but he has enjoyed traveling with the quartet for the past several years. Now that their quartet gig is over, it looks like the application may proceed smoothly. Hopefully as soon as he gets back from Montana."

The search of the bomb site at the Embassy quickly convinced the ATF agents of the identity of the bomb-makers.

"Hercules Unigel Tamptite dynamite. DuPont Tovex watergel explosives and electric blasting caps. Same signature as before," concluded Greg.

Destruction at the Embassy had been huge, six floors provided evidence of damage to walls, doors, and elevators. Once again, no one had been injured. Once again, no one seemed to have heard or seen anything suspicious. But the fingerprints were right there in the materials used for the bombs. The May 19th group, America's all-female terrorist organization, had struck again.

CHAPTER FIFTEEN

BROOK SPENT HOURS PREPARING for the sermons he would preach during the week of revival in Elk Lodge. The two messages he shared with congregations during their years of touring consisted mainly of extended illustrations he memorized in speech class. "The Song on Page 154" told the story of blind poet Fanny Crosby who wrote the hymn *Rescue the Perishing*. The words to that song motivated a man who ran a rescue mission in the eastern states. Each verse meshed with the account of a drunkard named Scotty who came to the mission and through conversion experienced rescue from addiction. When the minister eventually conducts Scotty's funeral, he is amazed to find that Scotty has been buried right next to the tomb of Fanny Crosby. People loved that story.

His other sermon included a supposedly true account from the Civil War. A young boy enlists as a drummer, and because of injury, faces amputation of one of his legs. His witness to the attending physician causes that man to accept Christ after the boy dies. The story was a real tear-jerker. Brook planned to use both sermons later in the week, but he couldn't just repeat them like he did when they were on tour with a different audience each night. He had to come up with something new.

Ron, Will, Cynthia, and Penny canvassed the entire town with flyers announcing the meetings. Stopping at the town office to post a flyer, the mayor called them into his office. To Ron's amazement, one of the Certain Sounds Quartet records played on his stereo. The cover occupied a prominent place on the table behind his desk.

"That you playing the piano, son?" The mayor leaned back in his chair, resting his boots on the corner of the desk. "Always been partial to southern gospel. It's just like country western without the honky-tonk. Do you know what you get if you play country western records backward? You get your truck back, you get your girl back, you get your dog back."

Laughing loudly at his own joke, he pointed to the chairs and waved them into a seated position.

"Bet you're wondering where I got this here record."

Without waiting for a reply, which he didn't seem to need in order to continue his one-sided conversation, the mayor continued. "You heard of Johnny France, the sheriff over in Madison County? Well, Johnny got it from the preacher in Ennis, and when he heard you were coming here to Elk Lodge, he sent it to me. I have a proposition."

The four of them looked at one another, wondering if they should respond, but it wasn't necessary.

"Cynthia Freeborn? Right?" The mayor jutted his chin in her direction. "Really appreciate your dad working with us to make room for the Fourth of July Rodeo Stampede this week. Not meeting on Independence Day was a gracious move. Like to return the favor."

Dropping his feet to the floor, he leaned over the desk in Ron's direction. "The rodeo includes a game feed during the supper hour. Elk, venison, moose, even rattlesnake. People love it. Just love it. Wondering if you might be willing to tickle the ivories during that meal. We'll move a piano into the school gym. People will love it. Just love it."

Before Ron could even blink, the mayor grabbed the telephone from its cradle and started to dial. "Good. It's settled then. I'll just call the *Outlook* and add that to the rodeo schedule. Do you take requests? I'm sure you do. I heard tell you even know some of those classical pieces like Bach and Beethoven."

Holding the receiver up into the air to let them know someone answered, the mayor continued as if whoever was on the line had been part of the conversation all along. "Ezra. I have Ron Freeborn here, you know, the pianist? Just arranged for a concert during the game feed. Add that to the day's activities, would you? I'll be in for an interview later on. Need to play this up big, right? Right. People will love it. Just love it."

Back on the street, Ron laughed in amazement. "Can you say railroaded?"

"I can certainly see why he's in politics." Penny shook her head as if to clear out the cobwebs.

"No one has ever been tempted to run against him," agreed Cynthia. "They call him Steamroller."

"Do you take requests?" asked Penny in a perfect imitation of the mayor.

"I guess I do now."

The mayor's interview with the *Outlook*, an entire half-hour on KELK Radio dedicated to cuts from the Certain Sounds album, and the flyers left in every screen door in town, produced the desired effect. Extra chairs brought down from the first floor of the library to the basement provided seating for the crowd filling the space where Rev. Freeborn's church had met since its inception.

Ron's prelude included old favorites he was sure everyone would recognize even if they were newcomers to church. *When the Saints Go Marching In*, *Amazing Grace*, and *Jesus Loves Me*.

Brook prepared for the service using the same technique which worked for him on tour. He wrote a story.

"Jonah was a preacher in a nice little church in Israel where he had a good work going," he began. "They were running two hundred in Sunday School, and everyone was tithing so he didn't have to worry about his salary. We see from verse one of the book of Jonah that he was pretty well off, because he was relaxing, just sitting back and taking it easy. The Lord had to tell him to 'arise.' Once the Lord got him up on his feet, he hit Jonah with a special message."

"You have a nice little church here, Jonah." Brook's bass voice dropped an octave in his best imitation of a message from the Divine.

"Yes, we do, said Jonah. There are only about a thousand people in town, and you can see our attendance on the board there. Pretty sharp."

"Jonah, I know about a large place nearby where they don't have a church. And they need one, because they are very wicked." Brook looked around wildly as if trying to find the location of the voice, letting people know that God could not be seen.

"The Lord really had his attention now, but not in a good way. Suspicion set in. He had no desire to go to Las Vegas, the wickedest place he knew."

"Where might that be, Lord?" Brook's voice quavered and he made his knees shake so people would know he was frightened.

"Nineveh."

The dialogue with God was over, so Brook reverted to his own voice.

"Jonah panicked. I tell you he really panicked. Nineveh sits over in the Tigris-Euphrates River Valley in present day Iraq, about five hundred miles east of Israel. Do you know the location of Tarshish? It's in Southern Spain, 2,400 miles west of Jonah's church. One of Jonah's excuses for not going to Nineveh would be how far away it was, but his decision to run would carry him even further away. He figured God would never find him over in Tarshish."

Brook sat in a chair facing the audience and began to jerk up and down, imitating the movement of a train like the actors did in *Music Man*.

"So, early the next morning Jonah caught a train ride to Joppa and purchased a one-way ticket to Spain. Confident that he had pulled one over on God, he made up for a lost night's sleep by curling up on a bench in the cruise ship and catching some z's. When the storm came, he didn't even wake up until the crew identified him as the culprit and threw him overboard." Brook fell off the chair and landed on the floor. "You know, God could have prepared an air-conditioned fish with interior decorating, a land-scaped throat, and a picture window, but He didn't. Even with such mighty uncomfortable accommodations, Jonah proved stubborn. It still took him three days to come to his senses."

Brook rolled into a crouched position, wrapped his arms around his knees and rocked back and forth as if seasick.

"Finally, after sloshing around in the half-digested juices of a fish's belly, Jonah did what he should have done in the first place. He prayed. God's answer came immediately. Let's just say that it involved regurgitation and an abrupt landing on shore. It certainly taught Jonah a lesson. Let's talk about what we can learn from Jonah."

During his preparation that week, Brook made certain he had enough material for a half-hour sermon. To his amazement only twelve minutes passed before he ran completely out of anything to say. Short of starting the story over again, he was done.

Pastor Freeborn stepped to the front of the room.

"Thank you, Brook. Wouldn't it be great to see the same kind of revival they experienced in Nineveh here in Elk Lodge? We'll be meeting every night this week with the exception of Wednesday during the rodeo. But we are pleased to announce that the mayor invited Ron to play during the game feed that night. As you meet others at the rodeo and invite them to come to the meetings, remind them that they can hear the same music each evening here at the library, as well as Brook's preaching. Ron, maybe you could play something for us now, maybe even take a few requests."

Cynthia and Penny covered their mouths to keep from laughing when he said that, but Ron managed to keep a straight face and simply nodded. Will stuck his hand in his mouth to prevent his giggles from surfacing.

Since services usually lasted an hour, Ron knew what his uncle had in mind. He was trying to cover for Brook so folks wouldn't be so aware of the abbreviated length of his first sermon. Sitting down at the keyboard he launched into the arrangement of *I'll Fly Away* which he had played at the National Quartet Convention. As soon as he was finished, someone called for *Moving Up to Gloryland,* and then *You Can Walk on the Water.* People requested familiar hymns like *The Old Rugged Cross* and *Count Your Blessings* next.

After almost thirty minutes of music, Pastor Freeborn stood up to pray and dismiss the crowd. Before he could ask people to bow their heads, a voice from the back of the room called out "*Yellow Rose of Texas.*"

A nod from his uncle prompted Ron to start playing the old cowboy tune even though he realized it was not completely appropriate for a church service. He knew James had a reason for acknowledging the request.

After the service concluded, Penny joined him on the piano bench. "Do you know who that was?"

He shook his head, figuring she had to be talking about the voice from the back of the room.

"That was my dad. He came to church. That's the first time since mother died. I'm so glad you knew *Yellow Rose.* That's what he called her."

Ron grabbed her hand and pulled her to her feet. 'Let's go. I'd love to meet him."

They made their way slowly through the crowd, many of whom wanted to thank him for his performance. By the time they reached the door to the outside, Lee Whitman had disappeared. Instead, Cynthia called to them from the top of the steps leading up to the main floor of the library.

"Penny. Ron. Come here. You have to see this. Miss Fenton got a new computer and Phil helped her get it working. You can ask it questions and play games and even send mail to people without stamps."

Phil had positioned Miss Fenton at the keyboard in front of the TRS 80 while he looked over her shoulder. "You won't break anything," he assured her. "Just type in that code they sent you, and you'll be connected to Altair."

"The email program you installed?" The librarian's fingers hovered over the keyboard as if touching it might cause something to explode.

"Right. You will be connected directly to the office in Helena and can leave them a message which they will see immediately."

"It all seems so impossible. Maybe I should just call them with my question."

Phil tapped her lightly on the back of her hands to encourage her. "Just go ahead and type. It's completely safe."

Cautiously she lowered her fingers, watching in amazement as the words appeared on the screen. "You're sure they will get this in Helena as well?"

"They will see exactly what you see here, I promise you. It's as if you are typing right on their computer."

Ron and Penny joined Cynthia and Phil as he continued to give instruction. The idea that written communication could be instant amazed them all.

"Can she only connect with the library in Helena?" Ron asked.

"Not at all. This computer can talk to any other computer in the entire world, as long as they both have the same software. In this case, Altair Basic. That's the beauty of the World Wide Web."

"So, I could write to my dad in Washington?"

"Does he have a computer?" asked Phil.

"At work he does. He's Deputy Director of the ATF."

"ATF? Then all you would need is an email address."

Miss Fenton pushed her chair back from the desk, seemingly glad to come to the end of her computer lesson. "I think I'm too old for this new-fangled equipment, kids. Maybe I'll just go back to regular mail."

As they watched, words began to appear on the screen as if by magic. Someone in Helena responded to her message. Seeing the words, she pulled her chair back up toward the screen and watched as the response to what she had just sent scrolled down the page.

"And then again, maybe not. This is exciting."

ALMOST THE ENTIRE CROWD in the basement of the library cleared out before a young boy standing patiently to one side of the room approached Brook.

"Mr. Wilson? I just wanted to stay long enough to tell you that I did it."

The boy appeared to Brook to be no more than fourteen. Long, gangly legs supported the rest of a body not mature enough to manage his growth spurt. His hair suggested styling with a brush-through of fingers rather than a comb. But a look of sincerity on his face immediately caught Brook's attention.

"Just Brook, kid. Mr. Wilson's my Dad. What is it that you did?"

The boy grinned. "Just what you said. I repented of sins."

It seemed as if the conversation had come to an abrupt end. Brook waited uncomfortably for a time and then tried to move things along. "Sins?"

One side of the boy's lip came up in a half smile. "Do I need to list them for you? Is that part of the deal? I already told them to God."

"Yes," Brook said, and then quickly, "No. You don't need to confess them to me. It's great that you told God. When did this happen?"

"While you were preaching. I repented, just like you said. I accepted the substitute God provided and allowed Him to carry the burden. That's what you said to do."

Brook honestly couldn't even remember saying those words, but he decided he must have. The kid wouldn't make something like that up.

"That's great, kid. Really great. I'm so glad you told me. By the way, I shouldn't keep calling you kid. What's your name?"

A smile from both sides of the mouth preceded his response. "Are you frank?"

A puzzled look crossed Brook's face before he answered. "I certainly try to be. Is there something else you needed to tell me?"

"Nope. But if you'll be Frank, I'll be Earnest."

And he was gone.

CHAPTER SIXTEEN

CLOUDS FROM THE WEST descended on Elk Lodge just as the revival meeting concluded on Tuesday night, sending everyone scrambling for their cars or milling around the basement until the rain subsided. After a stormy night, the sun greeted those arriving early for the rodeo the next day with a brilliance reflected off the fresh dusting of white snow capping the mountain peaks. Brook and Ron caught a ride to town with Penny and joined the Freeborns at the breakfast table. Elizabeth added new plates, and Will ran to the next room to bring more chairs. James passed them the waffles and syrup.

"Are you ready to ride today?" asked James as Brook piled waffles onto his plate. "Penny told you about our tradition out here in the west, didn't she? Every person who attends a rodeo for the first time is required to participate in at least one event. We've signed you up for steer wrestling."

Brook lathered his waffle with syrup, certain that he had never eaten better in his entire life before coming to Montana. He didn't even look up to see if Pastor Freeborn had the lop-sided smile on his face which indicated another joke. By now he knew banter could be expected anytime James stepped out of the pulpit.

"Sounds good to me," he said before stuffing a large slice of warm waffle into his mouth. "What did you do in your first rodeo go-around, mutton-busting?"

James laughed. "You got me there. The only event limited to those seven and under. Will doesn't even qualify for that six-second ride."

"Maybe we can convince Phil to register." Cynthia passed the waffles to Ron. "He doesn't know how to take you yet, Dad. I don't think he's ever met a preacher with a sense of humor."

"I hope his Fiat will make it into town," said Brook. "Penny suggested he ride with us in her Jeep this morning since the road still had some pretty good mud holes left from last night's rain. But he was messing with something in his trunk and said he'd come on his own. I have no idea what he carries in the trunk of his car, but he's out there every day moving it and sorting it and turning the boxes over. Not sure why he doesn't just unload it and take it into his cabin. I offered to help him one day and he acted like I was going to steal from him or something."

"Penny was certainly in a hurry when she dropped us off." Ron tried to keep his voice casual. "I thought maybe she would come in for breakfast." He knew they would tease him unmercifully if he let them see his disappointment at how quickly she had hurried away.

"She's leading the competitors into the arena carrying the American flag," explained Cynthia. "As Queen of Elk Horn Fourth of July Rodeo, that's her job. They'll choose a new queen tonight."

The Fourth of July Rodeo in Elk Lodge nearly tripled the population of the small town. Ranchers from Idaho, Wyoming, and Montana joined tourists visiting Yellowstone Park who wanted to witness an authentic western rodeo. High school bands from West Yellowstone, Ennis, and as far away as Bozeman marched in the parade down Main Street and out to the Rodeo grounds before bussing away to participate in their hometown Independence Day events. The local school band provided entertainment at the stadium between Bareback Riding, Team Roping, Barrel Racing, and Bull Riding events.

The sight of Penny on Jupiter holding the American flag and racing around the arena during the opening ceremony nearly brought Ron's heart up into his throat. She wore a bright orange vest fringed with white and decorated with stars and horseshoes. A blue bandana around her throat carried the star theme even further. Wrangler jeans hugged her hips and descended into beautiful gray cowboy boots with a white embroidery glow.

"Shyanne's," whispered Cynthia in his ear as he watched Penny and her horse circle the arena at high speed and then slow down to lead the other contestants around again at a more sedate pace.

"Shyanne's?"

"The boots. From Boot Barn. She'll wear a different pair when she competes. This outfit she wears just for show."

Ron thought he could certainly appreciate the show. She was without a doubt the most beautiful girl he had met on all their stops over the past four years. From the top of the black cowgirl hat decorated with diamond bling to the soles of her boots, which he now knew were Shyanne's, no other girl even began to compare with Penny Whitman.

The voice of the announcer echoed over the loudspeakers. "Welcome to the sixty-seventh Elk Lodge Stampede. Leading our Grand Entry today is none other than our own Rodeo Queen, Penny Whitman. Let's all stand as the high school band, under the direction of Merton Fields, leads us in the *Star-Spangled Banner.*"

"That's Penny's dad on the mic. He placed third in the nation in calf roping before losing his arm in a freak accident. Probably knows more about rough stock than any other man in the three-state area." Cynthia didn't whisper this time. Instead she provided color commentary for both Ron and Brook as the day progressed.

"Bareback riders start with their feet above the horse's shoulders, otherwise they are disqualified for not marking out the horse properly. He can't touch the equipment, himself, or the animal, with his free hand during the eight-second ride. Even so, the horse's performance counts for half of the total score. This afternoon will feature preliminary rounds. Riders with the best scores and times compete for the championship after the wild game feed."

When Penny raced out of the chute at full speed and traced a cloverleaf pattern around the barrels, Ron jumped to his feet to cheer. It seemed as if everyone else in the stadium joined him, and she and Jupiter responded to the excitement of the crowd.

"13.8 seconds," her father called out over the loudspeakers. "We'll see Penny again in the championship round this evening. She's already qualified for the Helena Stampede, and no doubt will be representing Montana at The National Finals Rodeo, known popularly as the 'Super Bowl of Rodeo.' The NFR determines the world champion in each of rodeo's main events: calf roping, steer wrestling, bull riding, saddle bronc riding, barrel racing, bareback bronc riding, team roping, and steer roping. The rodeo showcases the talents of the nation's top fifteen money-winners in each event as they compete for the world title. National Finals have been held in Oklahoma City since 1964, and this year they will be the site of an appearance by Elk Lodge's own champion, Penny Whitman."

With that announcement, the crowd stood to their feet, hooting, hollering, clapping, and stomping their feet in appreciation of their hometown hero. Her rodeo feats had become Elk Lodge's claim to fame. Four years of competition since high school produced enough ribbons to paper the walls of her bedroom. Victories at the Calgary Stampede, Cheyenne Frontier Days, and the National Western Stock Show contributed blue ribbons and huge belt buckles to her collection. She moved into the top fifteen early in the season that year, and the hometown folks gladly joined Lee in his prediction of a National Finals ride that would put Elk Lodge on the map later that summer.

The break for the evening cookout followed the barrel racing semifinals. Ron wasn't sure anyone listened as he played the piano in the high school gymnasium during the meal, but the mayor couldn't have been prouder. He stood right next to the piano, live on the air over KELK Radio, and after every number called on folks to bring their requests to him. The tables filled up quickly, and many sat in the stands holding plates of venison, elk, or moose on their laps while corn on the cob tried its best to roll off the sides of the paper plates. Every time Ron thought he might sneak away and try some of the wild game himself, the Steamroller called out another song title. Thankful for the ability to play by ear, he responded to requests for everything from *Sweet Beulah Land* to the *Beer Barrel Polka*. What he really wanted to do was to find Penny, but instead he nodded every time the Steamroller announced another title and provided accompaniment for the buzz of conversation in the roomful of diners.

WITH THE ENTIRE TOWN involved in the rodeo events, Phil found it easy to pick the lock on the basement door of the library and climb the stairs to the reading room. Good fortune shined on him when Cynthia asked him about helping the librarian with her new computer. Long-distance phone calls back to Washington often proved impossible, and he desperately needed to contact Louise. The dynamite in his trunk had started leaking even though he kept it dry and moved it around each day just like he had been told. Nitroglycerin oozed from the cylinders, frightening him every time he shifted the position of the containers. Just driving the Fiat over the road between town and the ranch terrified him. Every pothole he hit warned of potential danger. If the Organization was going to send the additional materials they promised, it needed to be done soon.

Gaining access to the computer made contact possible. His coded message to the email address he had been given could be sent safely. Rather than giving them his address at the ranch, which might have caused problems, he instructed them to send the box to him in care of the library. He figured that having the box delivered there would help direct the attention of anyone who was curious to the librarian instead of to him. In order to create even more suspicion, he added another email to the sent box using some of the language they included in all their communiques: "Down with Reagan. Defeat U.S. Imperialism."

He had finished typing and closing Altair when he heard a key rattle in the front door. Checking quickly to see that everything on the desk looked the same as when he arrived, he headed for the basement, and then stopped. It had to be the Fenton lady. The "Closed" sign on the front door and the fact that she had a key proved him right. Phil knew she couldn't be the one to discover those messages. She might report them to someone in Helena. He planted the message so others would find it and suspect her of writing it. She knew little about computers but having her find the email wasn't a risk he could take. Instead of making his escape, he hid in the stacks and watched. If she left the computer alone, he could relax. If she checked for email, another plan would be needed. Too bad she hadn't just stayed at the rodeo.

A cardboard box sat on the edge of the checkout desk, and he watched as the librarian placed several books into the box. Closing the lid, she taped it shut and carefully filled out a mailing label. Must be inter-library loans, Phil thought. She must have used the supper break in the rodeo activities to finish an uncompleted task. Now if she would just head back to the game feed at the gymnasium, he could slip out the back door and make his appearance there as well. No one would be the wiser.

Lifting the box as if to gauge its weight, Miss Fenton started for the door, keys in hand. But then she set it back down, seated herself in front of the computer and proceeded to type. Phil crept closer through the stacks and peered between books to watch as she opened Altair. The message he had just sent appeared on the screen. Shaking her head in a puzzled fashion, she appeared to read it several times before closing the window. Picking up the box once again, she walked out the door and turned back to insert her key into the lock. Before the door could be secured, it opened again as Phil stepped through.

"Could I help you with that box, Ma'am?"

A very surprised Miss Fenton stepped back slightly so as not to be hit by the door as he opened it.

"Phil? Where did you come from?"

Pretending to follow up his gentlemanly offer by taking the box from her hands, Phil shifted the weight of the box toward the steep stairs while at the same time placing a well-aimed kick toward the woman's knee. Off balance already from avoiding the door, she flailed and fell headfirst down the stairs, still clinging to the box and bouncing on each step as she fell.

Looking around to make sure no one had noticed, Phil re-entered the building, scooted down the stairs to the basement, and drove carefully back toward the gymnasium. Once there, he made certain Cynthia and Will and their parents saw him eating a barbecued elk sandwich.

The evening program proved even more exciting under the lights. Penny bested her afternoon score to win the Barrel Racing prize. She rode Jupiter up to the judge's booth to collect her prize and then turned him back to face the arena as her father handed her his microphone. The loudspeakers howled briefly as the cord extended, but then mimicked the hush which settled over the crowd. None of the other winners chose to address them in this way.

"First of all," Penny began. "I want to offer a warm thank you to all of you here in Elk Lodge and Gallatin County who supported me throughout my year as rodeo queen. I hope to do you proud in Oklahoma City."

That statement set off another standing ovation as the crowd yelled and stamped out their approval. When the noise began to level off, Penny continued.

"As most of you know, I am a proud member of the Big Sky People, known as the Arapahos. My ancestors included many of the first residents of this Big Sky Country we call Montana. We love our heritage, and we love our state. We want to see a prosperous future for all Montanans, Natives and newcomers alike. That is why I am choosing today, here on Independence Day, among my friends and neighbors, to announce my candidacy for Governor of the Great State of Montana. Alicia Walks-Softly has agreed to serve as my campaign manager."

This time the crowd thundered like the hoofbeats of a thousand braves riding Appaloosas into battle. A full ten minutes of cheering rocked the stadium as Penny handed the microphone back to her father and circled the arena waving her Stetson and demonstrating the bow Jupiter had perfected in front of each section of the stands. As she finally exited through the gates at the end of the arena, Lee introduced the next event. But nothing through the rest of the evening could top the announcement she made.

One of the bull riders got bucked off and ended up under the hooves of almost a ton of Brahman, but the clowns immediately raced over to catch his attention. The bull chased them into their protective barrels while the rider stumbled safely toward the fence and climbed over. The crowd cheered his narrow escape and then waited for the next rider to attempt the most dangerous eight seconds in sports.

After dark, the fireworks began. The lights in the arena darkened and Penny joined Ron, Brook, and the Freeborns in the stands. As the sun disappeared behind the Gallatin Mountains, fuses lit in a field behind the arena ignited pyrotechnics. Rockets exploded high above the stadium. Roman candles and a fountain blossomed nearer the ground. Catherine wheels crackled and whistled as they spun in right coils. Under cover of the darkness and the oohs and aahs of the crowd, Ron slipped a hand between him and Penny, catching her fingers in a loose grip. She didn't pull away.

The final set of rockets faded away into falling scraps of burning paper when they heard a siren in the distance.

"One of those burning scraps must have made it down to the ground," said Cynthia. "It happens every year. The fire department is always ready to put out the grass fires."

They didn't think any more about the siren until they walked into the house as the telephone rang.

"Freeborn residence," said James and then fell silent as the voice on the other end offered an extended message.

"I need to go to the hospital," he said as soon as the conversation was complete. "It's Miss Fenton. She fell down the steps in front of the library and suffered a concussion. They're not sure she's going to make it."

"Oh, no," gasped Cynthia. "May I go with you, Dad?"

James nodded, grabbing his car keys off the hook by the door. "Just hurry."

The desk clerk at the hospital recognized Pastor Freeborn and directed them to the emergency room. As they pulled back the curtain surrounding Miss Fenton's bed, they were surprised to find Phil seated by her bedside.

"Cynthia. Pastor Freeborn. I'm so glad you have come."

"Hello, Phil," said James. "Do you know what happened?"

"Just that she took a fall. Those front steps on the library are so steep. It's a real tragedy."

"It was necessary to use anesthesia because of the surgical procedures undertaken by her physician," explained her nurse. "We'll know more when she wakes up. For now, we just need to keep her under observation. The doctors have done all they can do."

Cynthia walked up to the bed and took Miss Fenton's hand as it lay on the blanket. "Could we pray for her, Dad?"

Pastor Freeborn place his hand on his daughter's shoulder and pulled her into a hug as he prayed, and Cynthia wept.

CHAPTER SEVENTEEN

BROOK PLANNED TO PREACH a sermon on Thursday night based on one of his favorite poems called "The Hell-Bound Train." The anonymous poet described vividly the journey of a drunken cowboy on his way to the place where "the imps torment you forevermore." He often used it on tour and never failed to get compliments on the recitation. For this sermon he wrote an additional episode where he stepped off the train and interviewed individuals already confined to the lake of fire.

Miss Fenton's accident the previous night made him question the timing of his sermon schedule. It didn't seem quite appropriate to talk about death and hell when she lay in the hospital in a coma. He didn't want to suggest in any way that she was doomed, or even use her fall as an emotional tool to convince people to think about their own mortality. In his mind, something about that approach seemed morbid. On the other hand, he had worked on the sermon for several weeks and didn't have anything else ready except the message he planned for Friday night as a means of wrapping up the week of revival meetings. So, after the song service and a rousing rendition of *Battle Hymn of the Republic* on the piano, Brook launched into the first lines of the poem.

"A cowboy lay down on the barroom floor
Having drunk so much he could drink no more.
So, he fell asleep with a troubled brain
To dream that he rode on a hell-bound train."

Half-way through the poem, just as the devil "capered about and danced with glee" shouting "Ha, ha, we're nearing hell," Brook jumped off the low platform and started his own descriptive story.

"See the flames leaping up from the lake of fire? We can smell the burning flesh and the singed hair, and yet everyone seems to be alive and conscious. The landscape consists entirely of rock, yet strangely enough the rocks burn like coal. Even the air appears to be on fire. Let's see if we can get the attention of one of the inhabitants and talk to him."

Walking toward the side of the room he waved an arm toward an invisible character. "Hey there. That's right, you. Come over here. We want to talk with you."

After shouting to get the man's attention, he lowered his volume to a more conversational level. "You must have been terrible up there on earth, a thief or something."

Changing the pitch of his voice and twisting his face into an evil expression, Brook assumed the character of the man in hell.

"Not at all," he growled. "I was a preacher."

"A preacher? I can't believe that. You certainly didn't preach about Jesus Christ."

"Jesus Christ?" The character he played sneered. "Don't mention that name. I heard him preach, saw him heal the sick and give sight to the blind. I told others about him. I was one of the twelve chosen by him to be his disciples. And now I have these pieces of silver in my hands and I can't get rid of them. I've thrown them away time after time, but I can't get rid of them. I can't get rid of them. They're driving me crazy. I keep remembering his face. I can't get rid of them."

"Go, Judas Iscariot, back to your eternal habitation, back to the blackness of darkness forever."

Brook pointed a finger toward the far wall and followed the imaginary Judas with his eyes as he faded back into the distance. In quick succession he moved on to other interviews. He talked with the rich man who begged God to send messengers back to his five brothers so they wouldn't come to the place of torment. King Agrippa came to life in his imaginative description of the man who was "almost" persuaded to accept Christ. His final interview involved a young person in modern-day America who, though raised in church, never made a personal decision to accept the Lord. His conclusion returned to the story of the cowboy on the hell-bound train.

"Then he prayed as he never had prayed till that hour
To be saved from his sin and the demon's power,
And his prayers and his vows were not in vain,
For he never rode that hell-bound train."

The crowd sat quietly while the pastor closed in prayer after leading them in a verse of *Just As I Am*.

Ron continued playing the final song quietly for a time as people began to leave, and then joined Cynthia and Penny who were visiting with Phil by the stairs leading up to the main library room. He came in on the tail end of some sort of argument.

"It's important, I tell you." Phil grabbed Cynthia by the arm, urging her to go up the stairs. "You have to see this."

"What's going on?" Ron stepped between the two of them. Phil had no business man-handling his cousin like that. Cynthia didn't seem to be struggling, but he still didn't like it.

"Phil just wants us to go upstairs and see something on the computer," said Penny. "He found something he says we need to know about."

Phil released Cynthia's arm, and Ron relaxed slightly as the four of them climbed the stairs. The computer screen glowed brightly as Phil took the mouse and scrolled up the page. An email message appeared, and they listened as he read it aloud.

"Down with U. S. Imperialism. Defeat Ronald Reagan. Protect the planet. Power to the people. Destruction is not violence if no one dies."

The email was signed: Caasi Mutali.

"Who sent this?" Cynthia asked.

Phil shrugged. "Had to be Miss Fenton. She's the only one with access to the computer. Did you notice who she sent it to? That's what caught my attention. ARU."

"Means nothing to me," said Ron.

"It would to your dad. The Armed Resistance Unit is the group that bombed the U. S. Capitol last fall. That's what the May 19th group calls themselves."

"You lost me there," said Penny. "May 19th?"

"They took the name because of the birthdays of two of their heroes. Malcolm X and Ho Chi Minh were both born on May 19. It's the only all-female terrorist group in the nation, an off-shoot of the Weather Underground."

"And you think Miss Fenton belongs to a terrorist group?" Ron stared at the computer screen as if some answer might appear out of the blue. Something didn't seem right about this, but he didn't understand enough about how computers worked to figure it out. He just couldn't imagine the librarian belonging to some east coast terrorist organization. Why would she be out in Montana if that was the case?

"Seems hard to believe, I know. But the evidence is right there in front of us," said Phil. With Miss Fenton unconscious in the hospital, he knew his conclusions couldn't be contested.

"Someone else could have sent the message," said Penny. "It didn't have to be her."

"Who? The library is only open when she is here." Phil pressed his point hard. "She's the only librarian.'"

"People come here during the services in the evening," argued Cynthia.

Phil shrugged. "That's true. But would any of them know how to send an email to someone?"

"Not me," admitted Cynthia.

"It's still hard to accept." Ron knew he didn't like Phil, but struggled with himself as to whether that constituted a reason not to trust him. He needed to talk to his dad, something he was pretty sure wouldn't fit with Phil's agenda.

Penny leaned over to read the message again. "Who is Caasi Mutali?"

"A pseudonym," said Phil. "They all use them. You didn't think she would sign her own name, did you? I think you should tell your dad, Ron. I could help you if you have an email address for the ATF."

Surprised by the suggestion, Ron turned and headed back downstairs. "Uncle James might know. I'll have to ask him."

CHAPTER EIGHTEEN

THE EMAIL PHIL SENT from the library in Elk Lodge initiated a chain of events in New York City. Now that they had an address, a small crate received careful attention and packaging. The contents had arrived just a few days earlier, and the recipients anxiously desired to send it on its way. Accustomed to the danger of living constantly surrounded by the materials necessary for the manufacture of bombs, that danger couldn't begin to compare to the uncertainty of harboring in their living room a dirty bomb from Russia.

As a result of their investigation of the bombing at the South African Embassy, ATF had been keeping an eye on what they thought might be a safe house for the May 19th group on the Lower East Side. Agents spotted three women loading a wooden crate into the back of a van identified as matching the description of a vehicle used in a recent robbery. Though unable to follow the van, they reported the activity to ATF headquarters. Judson and Greg arrived on the scene after a hurried trip from Washington with a search warrant, and discovered weapons, ammunition, bulletproof vests, and large amounts of stolen cash. Fingerprints remained the only evidence concerning those who had been living in the house.

Evidence of a hasty departure included wastebaskets overflowing with printed posters, letters, and flyers, some so fresh that the ink hardly had time to dry. The house obviously served as a publication center, armory, and bomb manufacturing plant.

"Nothing we haven't seen before," said Judson as they sorted through the mess. "Except this." He held up a bundle of papers. "How's your Russian?"

A feminine hand had apparently translated the heading. Barnadsky Institute of Geochemistry. The remainder of the writing still appeared in Cyrillic.

"Don't look at me," said Greg. "This is where we need your son. We can get it translated back in D.C. unless you want to send it out to him. You said he was in Montana, right?"

"Great idea. I'll put it in the mail as soon as we get back to the office. Maybe this will prove to be the break we've needed."

While the safe house submitted to ATF investigation, the van with the crate made its way to a UPS store in East Village. Two women unloaded the package and set it on the front desk.

"We need to send this to Montana. Will that be a problem?"

"Not at all," said the clerk, lifting the package and setting in on the scale. "UPS delivers anywhere. What's the address?" Shoving a mailing label across the counter, he watched as one of the women wrote in a careful cursive.

Caasi Mutali
County Library
Elk Lodge, Montana.

"How soon can you get it there?" The other woman seemed nervous, glancing back toward the door as if they might be interrupted at any time.

"Probably a week. We don't send packages to Montana very often."

The two women exchanged glances and nodded. "A week will work. But mark it fragile. Wouldn't want anyone dropping it along the way."

Their mission accomplished, the two of them returned to the van and drove away. East Village police found it abandoned and empty later that day.

After a long day in New York City, Judson and Greg returned to the Washington office. An email message printed out by a secretary awaited them on Judson's desk.

"I had no idea Ron even had access to a computer," he told Greg. "Or that he knew the address here. My brother must have given it to him."

"So, what does he say?" Greg poured himself a cup of coffee, anticipating another long evening.

"Not much. Just that a friend there in Montana found an email message from someone named Caasi Mutali which sounds a lot like the ranting communiques we've been getting from the May 19th group. Apparently, this friend thought I should know about it. He helped Ron forward it to us."

Greg stood over his shoulder and read the words off the paper on the desk.

"Down with U. S. Imperialism. Defeat Ronald Reagan. Protect the planet. Power to the people. Destruction is not violence if no one dies. Yup, sounds just like the other communiques. Maybe we should send those Russian papers to him by email now that you have contact."

"Are you offering to re-type them?" questioned Judson. "I'm not sure we even have a Cyrillic font on our computer."

"Right you are. Guess we'd better have it done in-house," admitted Greg.

"The rant sure sounds familiar, though. Of course, we've had reports of similar statements in both Los Angeles and Portland, so it may not be anything except some copycat. I don't want to worry Ron needlessly."

"Don't we have agents in that part of the country?"

"We do. But Montana covers a lot of territory. Why don't you check on contacts in that area? I'll write back to Ron requesting additional information. It won't hurt for him to keep his eyes open."

RON SLEPT RESTLESSLY THAT night, thinking about Penny's announcement and what her run for Governor might mean to their relationship. Waking early the next morning, he headed toward the barn, hoping to see Penny. They needed to talk.

Before he got to the barn, Phil spotted him and waved him over to the Fiat.

"Hey. Want to run into town and check to see if you have a reply from your father yet? I imagine the reverend has a key to the library he would loan us since he's been using the basement. We could check on the librarian and see how she's doing as well, if you like."

Ron glanced across the yard toward the barns but didn't see any indication Penny might be around. "Sure. Sounds like a good idea." Initial reluctance to leave the ranch faded as he realized this might be his best opportunity to get some answers from Phil. As they drove toward Elk Lodge, he started by referring to their earlier conversation during the trail ride.

"So, have you found anyone planning to drill here in southwestern Montana? I thought the big deposits were in the eastern part of the state and over into North Dakota."

"They are." Phil slowed down and did his best to avoid a rut in the dirt road, still worried about the dynamite in the trunk. "That doesn't prevent people like Secretary of the Interior Watts from opening up this area as well. If the Reagan administration has its way, nothing will be safe from exploration, not even Yellowstone."

"I seem to remember that Watts resigned last fall."

"Doesn't mean a thing," argued Phil. "His policies remain the agenda of the department. Rape the land, destroy the environment, all in pursuit of the almighty dollar. Did you know a House committee actually blocked his attempt to permit oil and gas exploration in another Montana wilderness area?"

"So, what makes you think he still has influence in Washington?"

Phil snorted. "Mainly because of his association with the religious right, like Falwell and the Moral Majority. He even claimed that we don't need to protect the environment because the Second Coming is at hand. And that from a man tasked with caring for public lands, one-fifth of all the land in the entire country."

Rather than coming to the defense of Secretary Watts, Ron pivoted the conversation in a different direction. He wondered just how far Phil would go with his ecocentrism.

"That sounds like Earth First rhetoric to me. Are you one of those guys who believes in blocking bulldozers and living in treetops to keep loggers from doing their work? Did you know the FBI considers the radical elements of the environmental movement the nation's top domestic terrorists?"

"Don't even get me started on the FBI. They label as terrorism anything which doesn't agree with their near-sighted, right-wing agenda. If it were up to the FBI, anyone who joins a protest march against apartheid or the Palestinian genocide would end up in jail. You can't call the protection of redwoods and wildlife terrorism. The real terrorists are those who deny the animal and plant kingdoms their equal rights. Destruction of property isn't violence if no one dies."

A STOP AT THE parsonage produced not only a key to the library, but an offer from Pastor Freeborn to accompany them. "I've been wanting to see this computer Cynthia talks about. I may have to look into getting one myself if it can do everything she says."

Phil turned on the computer and let it warm up before clicking on Altair Basic. He turned his seat over to Ron when the email from his father appeared, watching over his shoulder as he read.

"Thanks for the heads-up, Ron. Keep your eyes open. We have agents in the state, but it never hurts to be aware of what goes on around you. Your application for re-instatement to the Academy seems to be receiving good attention. I'll let you know as soon as I hear anything specific. Hope the meetings are going well."

"Do you want to reply?" asked Phil. He tried to remember what he had said about the FBI on their trip to town. No one ever mentioned the possibility that Ron had attended the Academy. He would have to be more careful what he said in the future.

"This is exciting," said James. "Is it like mailing a letter? Does it take time for the message to be sent to Washington?"

"Not at all." Phil sat back down in the chair and waited for Ron to dictate his reply. "Instant communication. The internet will change the world."

"Let's see," thought Ron aloud. "Tell him thanks for the update on the application. The meetings are going well. Tell him we've met one of the government agents from the EPA. We will certainly keep our eyes open and let him know if we hear or see anything."

Phil grinned to himself. The EPA fabrication was doing its job. It would be easy to keep track of messages from ATF as long as these dumb westerners depended on his computer expertise.

"Glad to help," he said, typing the message from Ron to the ATF.

CHAPTER NINETEEN

THE FINAL NIGHT OF the revival meetings brought out the largest crowd yet to the basement of the library. Ron played a half-hour piano concert before the start of the service, and Brook brought one of his well-practiced tour sermons. After the service Brook sought out the young man who introduced himself as Earnest and connected him with Pastor Freeborn. Although the attendance remained strong throughout the week with both the music and messages well received, the boy's decision remained the only public evidence of God at work during the revival.

James recognized Ernie immediately. He was one of Will's close friends and often visited in their home.

"What would you say to a weekly Bible study along with Will?" suggested Pastor Freeborn. "We could start with the Gospel of John."

"Does that come after Genesis?" asked Ernie. "Will loaned me a Bible after the service the other night, and I started reading from the beginning, but I can't say it made a lot of sense, especially when I came to all those 'begots.' A Bible study would be great."

"We will plan on it." Pastor Freeborn laid a hand on the boy's shoulder. "I am so glad to learn about your decision. Will and I have been praying for you. There's an index in the front of your Bible. Look up John and start reading there. I promise you there will not be any 'begots.'"

"WHERE DO YOU HEAD from here, Brook?" Cynthia handed a huge bowl of fresh popcorn to the young preacher as they sat around the living room at the parsonage after the meeting.

"Back home for a few weeks and then off to seminary," answered Brook. "Three more years in the classroom, unless I decide to go for a doctoral degree." He added more salt to his popcorn. "I know you went to seminary, Pastor Freeborn. I've been wanting to ask you a question. With all that training and far more years of experience than me, why did you invite me out for these meetings?"

"I've been wanting to know the answer to that too," grinned Ron, throwing a kernel of popcorn at Brook. "Seems like you could preach your own revival services, Uncle James."

James accepted his own bowl of popcorn and took a handful, chewing thoughtfully before answering. "One reason lies in the fact that I like to give young preachers a chance. They need the practice, and evangelistic meetings provide that opportunity. Penny here can tell you how many hours she spent riding her horse around barrels before she ever entered rodeo competition. The other reason comes from some advice an older preacher gave me. He said he always brought in an evangelist at least twice a year because it helped his people to hear the same lessons he shared, but from a different voice."

Brook followed up a mouthful of popcorn with a swig of root beer, realizing that salt had already been added in the kitchen. "That brings up another question. You just called me an evangelist and Ron used the term revival. What's the difference?"

"That's one of those questions you will find seminarians debating till the late hours of the night, Brook. For the most part, the two words are used interchangeably by the church of today. But here's my take on the matter. I think the evangelist mentioned in the New Testament looked more like what we would call a missionary. A missionary, or evangelist, like the Apostle Paul in the book of Acts, went to a particular location, shared the gospel, and organized converts into a church. What we call an evangelist today could be better termed a revivalist. He goes to a church which already exists and spends a week or so preaching to revive that group so they will do evangelism."

"I heard that Evangelist Billy Sunday didn't even give an invitation in his meetings until he had been preaching for several weeks," said Cynthia. "At least that's what Grandpa said."

"A good example," agreed her father. "Some of his campaigns lasted for ten weeks, something unheard of today. He would spend days encouraging the believers to invite their friends and co-workers and neighbors to hear him preach. Once that happened, he would call on those who came to respond to the evangelistic message. He was essentially a revivalist."

Brook swallowed his popcorn and took a swig of root beer. "So, you are saying that you are really the evangelist here in Elk Lodge and I have been the revivalist. I never thought of it that way before. Which brings up another question."

James laughed. "You are certainly ready for seminary, Brook. Your professors will be glad to welcome you. They like nothing better than answering multiple student questions and furthering the discussion with interrogations of their own. Shoot."

"Well, when we traveled for the college, the quartet sang at your church in Ohio. As I remember, on a Sunday morning seven or eight hundred people attended. Why did you leave a church like that to come here to the back side of nowhere?"

The room suddenly grew quiet. Elizabeth stopped in the doorway to the kitchen. Cynthia and Will sat down on the floor and looked at their father.

Embarrassed that he might have offended the Freeborns, Brook tried to retreat. "I'm sorry, pastor. That was probably out of line. You don't need to answer that."

Pastor Freeborn shook his head slowly. "No. It's fine. We just haven't talked about it for a long time. You probably realize already that ministry is not easy. When I was first called to that church, it seemed like a dream come true. They had a school the kids could attend. The salary offered to me was double what I had been earning previously. They provided a stipend which made it possible for us to purchase our own home instead of living in a parsonage. I don't know if you realize it, but most pastors never have the chance to build up equity in a home, which means they have no place to live when they retire."

"It was a dream come true." Elizabeth walked over to the couch and sat next to her husband, taking his hand in hers. "We just weren't awake."

"What I didn't understand when they called me as pastor was the culture of the area. The town depended entirely on auto manufacturing and glassworks for employment, and that meant everyone belonged to a union. When Ronald Reagan accepted the nomination for President, the issues seemed clear to me. Communism needed to be faced with strength because of the Cold War. Big government caused double-digit inflation and unemployment, and the answer of the Democrats always seemed to be higher taxes. The results of Roe v. Wade and the increase in abortions bothered me greatly. I avoided political sermons, but people knew when I joined the Moral Majority that I favored Reagan over the incumbent. I asked the church to help sponsor a Freedom Rally featuring the Sounds of Liberty."

"And no one opposed the Rally," said Elizabeth.

"No one opposed the Rally," repeated James. "But the murmuring began. People complained to deacons that they no longer felt fed by my sermons. Giving dropped substantially. One of the men, my strongest supporter when I first accepted the call to that pulpit, suddenly decided that he had unnamed philosophical differences with me. He didn't share them with me but had no problem discussing them with others in the church. I had decided early in my ministry that I would never be party to any kind of division in a church. I knew of too many church splits and wanted no part of such an experience. So, we announced our resignation and moved to Montana."

"We love it here," said Cynthia.

"For sure," echoed Will. "After all, if you change the spacing, no where becomes now here."

"What seemed to be disaster turned out for the best," agreed James. "Back in Ohio our church grew because of a reputation and programs attracting the attention of people moving to town. Here the growth has been a result of people who came to know Christ because they first came to know us. We operate a spiritual nursery, but new spiritual life makes for exciting discussions. One woman who started coming to church asked if the epistles were the wives of the apostles."

"That reminds me," said Brook. "When the young fellow I introduced to you tonight stopped me the night of that first meeting, we had the strangest conversation. He told me he repented of sin during the message, in response to something I don't even remember saying."

"The work of the Holy Spirit," nodded James. "I can't tell you how many times people have told me they heard something in a sermon which I didn't remember saying. I've never been one to wait until service time to ask the Spirit what to say. I am convinced He can work just as easily in my heart during the sermon preparation time the week ahead. If I put in my time in prayer and in Bible study, He has a way of using that readiness in ways I could never have anticipated."

"That wasn't all," added Brook. "When I asked him his name, he just said that if I would be frank, he would be earnest."

Will hooted. "Ernie Ernst. It's his favorite joke. He's weird."

"Now Will," his mother admonished. "You know better than to talk like that."

"Weird in a good way, Mom, like gnarly and radical. He's my best friend."

"The kid's a genius," added Cynthia. "He's taking senior Chemistry and Advanced Algebra as a freshman. The teachers don't know what to do with him for three more years of high school. I think he's ready for college."

"Thanks for following up with him, Brook. I plan to conduct a Bible study with him in the Gospel of John. Maybe after that we can help the school out by offering him some extra study in theology and biblical languages. What do you think, Will? Would he be interested in Greek?"

"He'd love it. Then he'd be a Greek Geek."

"Do his parents come to church?" asked Brook. "I didn't see him with anyone after the service."

Penny shook her head. "Ranchers like his dad and my dad attend church twice in their lives. Once when they get married and once when they get buried. The other night when Dad showed up at the service you could have knocked me over with the tail fin of a fingerling."

"Does that mean I am successful as a revivalist, getting people to bring others out to church?" Brook tossed a piece of popcorn back toward Ron who caught it with an open mouth. "Or did he show up just to see the pianist who has been courting his daughter?"

Once again, the room grew silent. Ron and Penny stared at the floor. Cynthia tried to mask her smile by stuffing her face with popcorn. She knew both her friend and her cousin wanted the visit to continue. She just wondered if either was ready to admit it in public.

Brook ignored the awkwardness, plodding ahead with his inquisition. "Are you heading back east with me, Ron? Or have you found some reason to stay here in Montana?"

"You could help with Boy's Brigade," suggested Will. "Teach us all those things you learned at the Academy, how to interrogate spies and disarm bombs and chase robbers through the streets at high speeds. I bet we could get all the fellows in town to come if they knew an FBI agent would be training them to shoot. No offense, Dad, but you're not the best shot in the world."

A look from Elizabeth finally succeeded in stopping Will's monologue, and the uneasy silence returned.

Looking over at Penny, Ron spoke hesitantly. "I think I'll stay for a while longer if it's alright with Uncle James and Aunt Elizabeth. Dad wants me to check on a strange message someone posted on the library computer. Besides, there's nothing waiting for me back east until I hear about my application to the Academy."

When no reaction came from Penny, he reached over and stole a handful of popcorn from her bowl, winking as she playfully pulled her dish away.

"Besides, someone offered to introduce me to more of the last frontier. There's still a lot of territory here in Montana to explore."

CHAPTER TWENTY

UPS DROPPED OFF THE crate from New York City at the end of a local route which extended to Elk Lodge from a hundred miles away in Bozeman, Montana. Cynthia noticed it on the library steps as she drove past on her way to the evening shift at the Elkhorn Café. A half-hour later when Penny and Ron stopped to return some books Penny had borrowed, the steps sat empty. A new librarian greeted them at the circulation desk. Her name tag read "Ethel Planck."

"Penny Whitman," the librarian read from the library card on top of the books being returned. "You must be from out at Ab-Sa-Ro-Ka Ranch. I know your father. I'm Ethel Planck from the State Library Association in Helena."

"Everyone knows dad," grinned Penny. "How is Miss Fenton doing?"

"As good as can be expected. Still in a coma, however. Who's your friend?"

Ron reached across the table to offer a handshake. "Ron Freeborn. Just to let you know, we've been using the library computer. Hope that's alright."

"That's what it's there for." Ethel grasped Ron's hand firmly with a true western handshake. "I don't imagine Frances used it much. She wasn't sure she even wanted one installed. It's an attempt by the Association to bring the entire state library system up-to-date."

"What I think Ron wants you to know is that he's not the only one who makes use of the computer, Miss Planck." Penny picked up her stack of books and nudged Ron in the ribs. "Tell her about the message, Ron."

"We really didn't mean to read someone else's correspondence. I guess email is new enough that I don't have a good grasp on internet etiquette. But this message popped up when I logged on."

Ron was uncertain how much to trust a person they just met, especially when they didn't know the truth yet about Miss Fenton's involvement with a terrorist group, or the relationship between the two librarians. He watched her face closely as he spoke, waiting for some subtle reaction, relying on his training at the Academy.

"I guess I should explain," he went on. "My father, Judson Freeborn, works for Alcohol, Tobacco and Firearms back in Washington. The message which popped up sounded similar to communiques from a terror group he has been investigating. Death to America and that kind of language. So, I forwarded it to him. He said similar statements have been associated with groups in California and on the east coast but did seem a little strange coming from here in Montana."

The librarian swiveled around to face the computer. "Do you think you could show me where you found the emails?"

Ron and Penny joined her behind the desk. "It was right there in the same program I used to write to my dad. I think Phil called it Altair." He took the mouse and scrolled through the inbox. His correspondence with ATF appeared immediately, including a copy of the email he had returned. But any evidence of use by someone named Caasi Mutali did not appear. He scrolled up and down the list, almost willing it to appear so he didn't look like he was lying.

"It was right here. We both saw it." Ron looked over at Penny who nodded agreement. "And my uncle, too, when we came back to retrieve the message from Dad. Phil, too. He's the one who first discovered the email."

"Phil?"

"Adams. He's staying in one of the cabins out at the Whitman's. The EPA sent him out here to investigate rumors about oil exploration near the Park."

"So, he's another person who has been using the computer?" After her lack of surprise when first hearing about the computer use, the librarian appeared to take this latest information far more seriously.

Ron answered slowly, trying to think back to the occasions when the messages had been received. "I guess you could say that. Phil is really the only person who has been using the computer. He's the only one besides Miss Fenton with any idea how it works. The rest of us are complete neophytes."

"I see. Do you think he would have had any reason to erase the message you saw?" The new librarian took the mouse from Ron and continued scrolling.

Ron and Penny looked at each other before he answered. "Not that I know. He has some pretty strong environmental views, but I guess that goes with the territory for the EPA. He doesn't like President Reagan, but he works for the government."

Ethel stamped Penny's library card and handed her the new books she had chosen. "Guess we'll just have to keep our eyes open like your father said, Ron. I appreciate your telling me about the computer use. Check back any time to see if you have any more messages from the ATF."

Penny and Ron climbed into her Jeep after the futile attempt to recover the missing email.

"Do you think she's the one who deleted the mail? Or Miss Fenton?" Penny seemed puzzled over the entire incident.

Ron shrugged. "I just can't believe that Miss Fenton would have anything to do with a terror group, but who else had access to the computer?"

"Didn't you see the message after Miss Fenton's accident?" asked Penny.

"That's right, I did. But I still don't know when it appeared. Phil and Uncle James and I saw it after the accident and before the arrival of this new librarian. But what do we know about this Ethel Planck? All we really know is that the group my dad has been investigating involves only women."

"Send her name to your dad," Penny suggested.

"On her computer, without her finding out? Correspondence with him through the library computer is probably not wise any longer. Maybe I should give him a call."

Penny started the Jeep and backed up to exit the parking lot when Ron laid a hand on her arm. Following the direction of his nod, she pulled up to the side of a dumpster. Lying on the ground, as if discarded in a hurry, lay an empty crate. The mailing label read Caasi Mutali.

Ron loaded the crate into the back of the Jeep, and they headed in the direction of the parsonage. Uncle James agreed immediately to let him make a call to Washington.

"Hello, Dad? I'll try to keep this short. I'm on Uncle James' phone and you know what it costs to call long-distance. Just wanted you to know that we found an empty box in the library parking lot addressed to the same person who wrote that email."

Penny and James couldn't hear Mr. Freeborn's reply, but they watched Ron's eyes grow wide as he listened.

"Nuclear? Do you think they did the translation correctly?"

Ron grabbed a pen off the desk and looked around wildly for some paper. James placed a pad on the desk as he started scribbling furiously, holding the receiver with his chin so the paper wouldn't move as he scratched.

"Zalery Varsukar," he said as he wrote. "Gorbachev. START treaty. SCLM. What do you want me to do?"

The writing stopped. Ron sat in silence as his father finished his communication, and then returned the phone to its cradle. Penny and James sat quietly as well, waiting for him to share what he had heard.

"It's possible the crate contained something radioactive." Ron exhaled the breath held in while listening to his father. "A dirty bomb. Dad doesn't know that for sure. Agents watching a possible safe house in New York spotted women loading a crate into a van. When Dad and Greg searched the house, they found a sheaf of papers in Russian. Apparently, researchers at the Barnadsky Institute of Geochemistry discovered a method for sensing gamma rays from a distance of ten kilometers. Gorbachev used the discovery to demonstrate how safely arms inspections could be conducted and convinced the United States to sign the START treaty. In the course of their research, the same scientists produced a small nuclear device they ignited with conventional explosives such as dynamite. A possibility exists that the crate the agents witnessed being loaded back in New York City contained such a device. He wants to know if you still have a Geiger counter, Uncle James."

CHAPTER TWENTY-ONE

PENNY'S ANNOUNCEMENT OF HER candidacy for Governor at the rodeo sparked a groundswell of support not only from the reservations, but across the state. Montanans showed pride in their history, including the role Native Americans played in the development of the state. Editorials in papers from Dillon to Plentywood embraced the idea of honoring one of their original peoples in that way. Although Governor Schwinden remained very popular and would prove difficult to defeat, Republican leadership reasoned that the landslide victory they anticipated on the national level would provide long coattails for state and local candidates. 1984 provided the perfect opportunity to offer a young, female, Native American as a prospect for Governor.

The Republican Party of Montana met for their convention at the Al Bedoo Shrine Auditorium in Billings. The national Republican Party's vision of America's future, the heart of their platform, began with a basic premise: "From freedom comes opportunity; from opportunity comes growth; from growth comes progress."

Ron took a seat toward the back of the auditorium and watched with pride and sadness as Penny joined the celebrities on the platform, including President and Nancy Reagan. Conviction that she would be nominated and serve the state well as Governor made him proud. Realization that her political success destroyed any hope for their future together produced sadness. She needed to remain in Helena, and he needed to return to the Capitol. An Arapaho politician wouldn't be happy on the East Coast. As much as he loved Montana, he couldn't imagine working outside the Beltway.

President Ronald Reagan, looking much younger than his seventy-three years, upheld his reputation as the Great Communicator, addressing in his folksy manner the very issues important to Montanans.

"When I took office in 1981," he began, "our economy was in a disastrous state. Inflation raged at 12.4 percent. The cost of living had jumped 45 percent in the Carter-Mondale years. The prime rate was 21.5 percent. Federal spending increases of 17 percent per year, massive tax rate increases due to inflation, and a monetary policy debasing the dollar had destroyed our economic stability. During that first term we brought about a new beginning."

The audience broke into applause as he delivered what had become one of the key sound bites of the election. "Americans are better off than they were four years ago, and we're still improving."

The accusation by the Montana Democratic Party that the administration planned to allow oil and gas development around and even in Yellowstone Park had headlined several of the state newspapers that morning. The President chose to address the matter directly.

"It is part of the Republican philosophy to preserve the best of our heritage, including our natural resources. The environment is not just a scientific or technological issue; it is a human one. Republicans put the needs of people at the center of environmental concerns. We assert the people's stewardship of our God-given natural resources. We pledge to meet the challenges of environmental protection, economic growth, regulatory reform, and enhancement of our scenic and recreational areas. While protecting the environment, we should permit abundant American coal to be mined and consumed. Environmentally sound development of oil and natural gas on federal properties, which has brought the taxpayers $20 billion in revenue in the last four years, should continue."

Almost as if he looked behind himself and saw the grimace on Penny's face concerning the one major area where she disagreed with the national platform, the President called out her name.

"What a privilege it is to commit my support to the candidacy of your next Governor, Penny Whitman."

The mention of her name ignited a carefully planned, spontaneous demonstration. Tom-toms began to beat in the back of the room and dancers rose from within the various county representations, spilling out into the aisles. For more than ten minutes the colorful display of masks, feathers, and shawls interrupted the President's speech. No one seemed to enjoy it more than Reagan. Moccasined feet repeated the intricate steps from a variety of Native dances. Elements of the grass dance, ghost dance, and hoop dance intertwined throughout the auditorium. As the demonstration wound down, the President led the applause and then continued his speech.

"Who knows better what Montana needs in the years to come than one of our Native Americans. We support the right of Indian Tribes to manage their own affairs and resources. Recognizing the government-to-government trust responsibility, we are equally committed to working towards the elimination of the conditions of dependency produced by federal control. The social and economic advancement of Native Americans depends upon changes they will chart for themselves. We urge the nations of the Americas to learn from our past mistakes and to protect Native populations from exploitation and abuse."

Ron hadn't anticipated attending the formal dinner that evening but found himself seated directly across the table from the President and Nancy as a guest of Penny. While they awaited the arrival of the executive party, waiters passed through the room carrying trays of smoked whitefish and salmon canapes. Once seated, plates of elk tenderloin, huckleberry salad, and morel mushrooms sautéed in butter awaited them.

Nancy Reagan immediately set everyone at ease.

"We are so excited that you are campaigning for governor, Miss Whitman," she said. "But I am curious about something. I know that as ladies we are not comfortable talking about age, but my husband handled that question quite well in the last debate, and you seem to be handling it just as efficiently. Would you mind explaining to Ronnie and me exactly what the law states here in Montana about the age question?"

"I loved your husband's response to Senator Mondale," Penny said. "I just hope that Governor Schwinden doesn't use the President's reply against me. Unlike your husband, he might just be tempted to exploit for political purposes his opponent's youth and inexperience. Montana law states that the Governor must be twenty-five years of age. That will be true when I take office in January, although it is not true today."

"And who is this young man providing your escort this evening? I take it you must have convinced him to vote for you as well as escorting you to this banquet."

"I'm sure he would if he were a citizen of Montana," Penny replied. "This is Ron Freeborn. He comes from your part of the country, Washington, D.C."

The President, engaged in a discussion with the man seated to his right, shifted his attention immediately to them.

"Freeborn? Ron Freeborn?" Reagan stood, reached across the table, and grasped his hand. "Young man, you are a legend inside the Beltway. Highest score ever recorded in Academy history, concert pianist, fluent in Russian, and banished from serving while on your way across stage to receive your badge. Director Webster told me about it himself. Felt bad, too, but had no choice. Executive privilege trumped his own personal feelings. What are you doing out here in Montana?"

"Now Ronnie," interrupted Nancy. "Is that any question to ask a young man sitting next to a beautiful young lady like Penny?"

"Guess you're right." The President beamed at his wife and resumed his seat at the table. "But we need men like you in Washington, Ron. We need men like you."

CHAPTER TWENTY-TWO

CYNTHIA STAYED TO CLOSE and clean up at the Elkhorn Cafe just as she did every Friday night since first employed. She thought nothing of walking out the back door at midnight to drive home. This was Elk Lodge, Montana, not New York City.

"Hello, Cynthia."

The voice from the shadows on the other side of her Jeep startled her, but still didn't cause alarm since she recognized it immediately.

"Hello, Phil. I didn't see you inside. Skipping your buffalo burger tonight?"

Phil opened the passenger door, climbed in beside her, and waved a pistol in her direction. Although she recognized his actions as abnormal behavior, she didn't panic. After all, Phil was someone she knew.

"I need your Jeep, Cynthia. My Fiat can't handle the rocks on that logging trail up to the old mine."

"Don't expect it can. I'll just drive home and hand you the keys there. You won't need to use the gun."

"Wrong. Can't have you tattling to the sheriff now, can I? Besides, I need a guide. I'm not sure I could find the mine in the dark. I need you to guide me to my destination. Understand?"

Cynthia nodded. It made no sense to argue with a loaded pistol. She needed to wait until a better opportunity for escape presented itself.

"Seems like a strange time to head up to the mine. Wouldn't it be better to wait until morning?" She turned right onto Main Street and headed south toward Whitman's ranch. The streets sat empty, and she knew it would only get quieter when they crossed the river. "I suppose you heard that Penny got the nomination."

"Sure did. I also heard that the Teflon President made an appearance here in Montana. Seems to be a likely time to create an October surprise, even though it's only July. We'll see how much Teflon it takes to deflect the blame for destroying Yellowstone Park as a direct result of his cockeyed plans to rape the land with oil and gas exploration."

"I always thought the goal of the EPA was to protect the environment."

Phil sneered. "Try ELF instead of EPA. The Environmental Life Force. The only way we can truly protect Mother Earth is to resacralize Western ideas about religion and capitalism. Sometimes you need to destroy the present to preserve the future. Have you read Abbey's *The Monkey Wrench Gang*? Small potatoes. Tree-sitting and spiking may save a few Redwoods, but it's going to take a major disaster to awaken the public to the destructive machinations of Reagan and his Republican cohorts like Watts. Did you know that Watts said protecting natural resources was unimportant because of the imminent return of Jesus Christ? How stupid can a person get?"

"Watts hasn't been Secretary of the Interior since October of last year, Phil. And besides, he didn't say that at all. Liberal reporters twisted his remarks. We checked it out in debate class. What he said was that he didn't know how many generations we can count on before the Lord returns, but that we need to manage the environment with skill to leave resources behind for those coming generations."

"Manage with skill? That's just jargon for destroying endangered species in order to line the pockets of Republican fat-cats with obscene profits from natural resources which belong to all the people, not just some pasty-white-face plutocrats." Phil lowered the pistol and laid it on his lap, convinced the young girl didn't plan to try any heroics.

"So, what's the plan? Are you going to ignite the super-volcano in the Yellowstone caldera and cover several states with three feet of volcanic ash in order to blame it on Reagan and hand the election to Walter Mondale?"

"Bingo. Except we won't need a super-volcano. The Fairweather mine extends into the park at the southwestern corner of the caldera. Even a small underground explosion will affect the Lower Geyser Basin and disrupt Old Faithful. No candidate could possibly survive an election after pulling the plug on Old Faithful."

Cynthia navigated the road south as slowly as possible. She figured she could blame it on the fact that she didn't want to hit a deer if he complained, but he said nothing about the slow progress. She could tell his trigger finger itched. He didn't relax even when they turned off onto the logging road and headed up toward the mine. She figured he was as tightly strung as a recurve bow.

"Actually, these so-called revival meetings your father organized have been an interesting addition to my education concerning the ludicrous nature of religion in America. It provided my first chance to observe fundamentalist ritual. Maybe you can help me see what anyone could possibly claim was revived during the week. A few people came to hear your cousin play the piano who wouldn't otherwise have been in church, but I can't see where that revived them in any way. All old man Whitman wanted to hear was *The Yellow Rose of Texas*."

Cynthia swerved to miss one of the boulders in the road. They seemed to grow larger the closer they came to the entrance of the mine. But they provided her with another excuse to slow down even more. "Have you ever heard of Charles Spurgeon?" she asked.

"Can't say that I have. Who is he? Another one of your evangelists?"

"Not really. He pastored the Metropolitan Tabernacle in London back in the 1800s."

Phil snorted. "I'm sure that must be relevant to life today."

"So, do you really want to learn something?" Cynthia snapped, tired of his callous attitude and sarcasm. "Or has your liberal education closed your mind to anything you don't already accept?"

"Girl, you have a smart mouth for someone who's literally under the gun."

"I'd quote Psalm 14 to you if I thought it would make any difference. That's the one where the Bible calls a man a fool who refuses to believe in God. But instead, let me tell you the story of Spurgeon. Charles was only fifteen when he got caught in a snowstorm and walked into a Methodist chapel for shelter. Sitting in the back row, he listened as an unidentified substitute lay preacher read a text from Isaiah 45:22, 'Look unto me, and be ye saved, all the ends of the earth; for I am God, and there is none else.' The speaker hadn't even prepared a sermon, so he just kept repeating that verse. Then, he looked right at Spurgeon, pointed a finger in his direction, and shouted, 'Young man, you look miserable. Look! Look! Look to Jesus. Look now.' I would just about bet that if you had been there you would have asked the same question you just asked me. How can anyone claim that anything was revived that snowy day?"

"Right you are, smarty pants. What possible good would it do to look to some ancient crucifix hanging on the church wall. So, what's the point?"

Cynthia took her eyes off the road and stared him down. "The point is that Charles Spurgeon got saved that day. He didn't look to a crucifix. He looked at the living Christ, risen from the dead, the only One who could save him. The entire course of the rest of his life became one of service to God. That's what revival is all about."

"And you think that happened again here in Elk Lodge, Montana? I must say, little girl. You have it bad. The best thing you could do is ditch this joint and get a real education. Columbia University would quickly straighten out your backwoods religious ignorance."

"I do think it may have happened here. One of Will's friends, Ernst Edwards, accepted Christ that week. He could very well grow up to be someone even greater than Charles Spurgeon."

"Poppycock. But then, I guess you'll never know. I'm sure you realize by now that I can't leave any loose ends. When the article about Reagan's goons creating a terrible accident by their unrestricted gas and oil explorations hits the front page of the *New York Times*, I can't risk anyone showing up with a contradictory story. Not even a high school debater from backwoods Montana. An accident in an abandoned mine will be even easier to arrange than a fall down the steps of the library."

Cynthia pulled the Jeep up to the edge of the large rocks surrounding the door of the mine and turned off the engine, pocketing the keys before Phil thought to ask for them. Raising the revolver, he nodded for her to open the door.

"Well, lookee here," he smirked. "I think we have arrived at our destination. Time to make the donuts."

CHAPTER TWENTY-THREE

NORMALLY THE SHERIFF OF Gallatin County, Montana, would have called Sheriff Johnny France of Madison County and organized a search and rescue operation when Cynthia Freeborn did not return home after her shift at the Elkhorn Café. However, both sheriffs and all rescue units had been called out earlier in the day because of the abduction of an Olympic runner from Bozeman named Kari Swenson. One man had already died trying to rescue her, and law enforcement from the entire southwestern region of Montana joined the search. Gallatin alone covered 2,600 square miles with Madison adding another 2.3 million acres, much of it mountainous and remote. Manpower stretched to the limit did not allow for another search to be mounted.

The discovery of the Fiat in the parking lot behind the Elkhorn Café provided some direction for the family and friends of Cynthia to launch their own investigation. Elizabeth and Will volunteered to search the town, while James and Ron headed south toward Ab-Sa-Ro-Ka. At the ranch, Penny and her father joined the search as soon as Phil's cabin proved to be empty.

"Reverend, the road on south of here goes all the way over the Continental Divide and into Idaho but remains quite accessible with a four-wheel drive. It's the only way out of here without heading back into town. Why don't you and I take Penny's Jeep and drive that road while the kids saddle up and check out the areas between here and Elk Lodge. If they have your daughter's vehicle, it's pretty certain they won't be too far away from one of those two trails."

"Really appreciate your help, Lee. We'll just have to cover as much territory as possible until law enforcement can release some of their planes from the Swenson search," agreed James.

The two men headed south as Penny tacked up the horses.

"Anything I can do to help?" asked Ron as she readied the saddles.

Penny threw a blanket over the back of her palomino and easily hefted the saddle into place. "Probably not. I'd love to teach you about horses sometime, but right now it's easier to just do it myself. Where do you think we should look for Cynthia and Phil?"

"I guess we're all just assuming that they are together," answered Ron. "He could just as well have left her somewhere in town and driven off in the Jeep by himself. For all we know he's on his way to West Yellowstone or into the Park. Planting a dirty bomb near Old Faithful would certainly accomplish his goal of disrupting the coming election if it could be blamed on Reagan."

"Then why take the Jeep? His Fiat would have no trouble navigating the roads between here and West Yellowstone."

"Just trying to consider all the possibilities. I do think he has both Cynthia and her vehicle. But why? Why not just steal the Jeep while she worked?"

Penny finished saddling her mount and then cinched up the bay for Ron. "Maybe he needed a guide."

"Of course." Ron slapped his forehead. "Why didn't I think of that. The logging road. Phil may be trying to follow that all the way into the park in order to avoid detection at the West Yellowstone entrance. He has no way of knowing how much information park rangers know about the intentions of his group. He knows that Dad said ATF would send out an immediate alert to all the agencies in Montana, but who knows whether that included national park employees?"

"It's a place to start. We'll find her, Ron. I know we will. Geronimo is ready. Let's head out."

Ron appreciated Penny's easy pace, not just because of his status as a greenhorn, but also because he didn't want to miss any possible marks indicating recent travelers. Even though his mind wrestled with the questions surrounding Cynthia's disappearance, he couldn't help but marvel at the abundance of wildflowers. Sunflowers he recognized, but the meadows glowed with a dozen other yellow blooms he had no ability to name. Pink, blue, and white flowers flowed through the narrow valleys like living streams of color. Forest-green Lodgepole Pines framed a grove of Aspens. A doe and two fawns blended in with the mottled brush, invisible until Penny pointed in their direction.

"It always amazes me how little mankind has affected this part of the country," he whispered, anxious not to destroy Paradise by alarming the deer.

"Mountains as old as time, plains wide as forever, and the blue sky flung across." Penny brought her horse to a standstill and gazed down at the logging trail. "That's the way A. B. Guthrie described Montana in *The Last*

Best Place. Look at this. See how the boulders are scraped and turned? A vehicle passed this way in the last few hours."

Ron stopped as well and looked where she pointed, seeing nothing different from the rest of the dirt in the road. His lack of expertise provided another reminder of her unity with a land he was learning to love but would never identify with in any consciousness comparable to hers. She belonged to the mountains, reflected the beauty of the wildflowers, shared affinity with the Aspens, and would wither away in the harsh atmosphere of Washington, D.C.

"I can't imagine anyone desiring to damage any part of this pristine landscape, especially for political reasons," he said.

"My people have been saying that for generations. We are guardians of the land which belongs to all peoples. From earliest times we have roamed the plains and mountains in search of deer, elk, and buffalo, never forgetting that the world is here for us to use but not to destroy. When we left for new horizons, we knew the sun would again rise over the land we were leaving. It needed to be ready for us when we returned."

"Uncle James says people will always return to Montana if they drink enough crick water."

What Ron wanted to say didn't fit at all with the words coming from his mouth. He wanted to talk about her being ready for him when he did return but sustained little hope of that ever happening. It would take a miracle for them to have a future, and so far, his life had been pretty short in the miracle category.

"Pastor's always saying that. I like to remind him the statement rings true unless the water contains giardia." Penny mounted her horse and led the way up the logging road. "In that case you'll probably get so sick you'll never want to see another mountain stream again. You'll require fluoridation and purification for every drink you take. Montana will become only a memory of Montezuma's revenge."

Like the earlier glimpse of the doe and fawns, Ron probably would have missed the Jeep hidden in the forest near the mouth of the Fairweather mine without Penny's keen eyesight. Even when they tethered the horses and approached on foot, he had to look closely to see it through the brush piled over the top. Once again, he thanked his lucky stars for the sharp eyes of his companion. Eyes that glowed with a light that made him want to kiss her. No other set of female eyes had ever done that. Why now? Why her? How could he leave her in Montana and return to the Academy? On the other hand, how could he stay if the appointment came through? If he ever did return for a visit because of the crick water, she would be Governor and he would have a job with the FBI in Washington. First the disappointment at graduation, then the break-up of the quartet, and now this. The Apostle Paul wrote that tribulation produced patience. God must be planning to make him into the most patient person the world would ever know. But he certainly didn't feel patient, which meant a whole lot more tribulation must be coming.

Resisting the urge to see if she might be amenable to a kiss, Ron dismounted. Approaching stealthily, they inspected the vehicle at the mouth of the mine. No Cynthia. No Phil. Abandoning that search, they looked toward the mouth of the Fairweather mine.

CHAPTER TWENTY-FOUR

THE SUREFIRE FLASHLIGHT PHIL carried had been an instant hit in the tactical world when it first appeared. Using a halogen bulb and high-density Lithium camera batteries, the SureFire illuminated the pitch-black darkness of the old mine with enough light that Phil and Cynthia could make their way through the fallen timbers without stumbling. In order to prevent escape, Phil tied a noose around Cynthia's neck, with one end fastened tightly to his belt. He bound her hands behind her back. Since his hands were full of the flashlight and the box, progress proved to be slow. Any attempt on her part to impede their movement brought pressure on the noose. She quickly learned that in order to keep breathing she would have to keep walking.

"You know this mine has been condemned for years," Cynthia ventured. "It isn't safe."

"According to old man Whitman, you mean. Just another attempt to keep people away from his property is what I think. Besides, by the time we plant this bomb and the dynamite, we won't be trespassing on ranch land. Yellowstone Park belongs to everyone, remember? Miners didn't abandon the Fairweather just because they were afraid of breaking into the geyser basin and flooding the mine with water. The government in Washington put pressure on them because they would be stealing natural resources from a national treasure. That's what makes Reagan such an environmental threat. He chooses to ignore decades of progress. All animals should be protected, not just those in the national park system. We are not superior to other living organisms or separate from other species."

"Including spiders and cockroaches, I suppose."

"Don't be a smart aleck."

"Isn't it possible that your concern for the environment might seem hypocritical if you are willing to destroy both the land and the animals just to prove some political point?" Cynthia found it increasingly hard to breathe but talking somehow relieved the tension. It made her captor seem a little more human.

Phil deliberately jumped over a fallen timber, jerked on the rope, and forced her to her knees, already bleeding from numerous falls.

"Don't you lecture me about hypocrisy. You so-called Christians have a lock on that title. Your Moral Majority is no different than the KKK. Just scumbags trying to shore up the dying system of capitalism through utilization of a racist agenda. If you want to see a classic example of hypocrisy, look at the Jewish massacre of Palestinians using the excuse of a non-existent holocaust. Or the Right to Life people who murder doctors and bomb abortion clinics. Zionism, fascism, killer cops, and Amerika's Koncentration Kamps qualify as hands-down winners when it comes to hypocrisy."

Cynthia struggled to her feet and twisted her neck in a futile attempt to loosen the noose. Every breath became an effort as she hovered on the edge of a complete blackout from lack of oxygen.

"Just another tenth of a mile to get to the edge of the caldera according to my calculations. Time to get this party started."

Untying the rope from his belt, Phil pushed Cynthia up against one of the side braces and looped the rope over a beam. Only then did he slip two fingers under the noose to give her some room to breathe. Next, he undid the knots holding her hands together and re-tied her hands to the wall brace.

"Now, don't go anywhere while I'm gone. There's plenty of length to my fuse to provide for my escape but any interference from you and I might just leave you here. Be a good girl and I'll take you with me on a trip into Canada."

Cynthia had no intention of being a good girl. As soon as Phil disappeared beyond a bend in the mine tunnel absolute darkness circled her, but she still started stretching the rope to get to the pocket of her jeans. Touch rather than sight was all she needed. She couldn't fathom why he had not searched her and taken her knife. He probably didn't think girls would carry such a weapon. It would have helped tremendously if she could have just scooted lower by bending her knees, but the noose prevented that alternative. The only choice she had was to stretch her fingers and curl her knees up toward her waist to bring the pocket as close as possible to her hand. Raising her knees put all her weight on the noose, which meant she had just one chance at success before choking to death. Curving her hands behind her back and stretching the bindings on her hands to the limit, she took a deep breath, jammed her right hand into the pocket, and grasped the metal loop on the end of her pocketknife. Slamming her feet back down to the ground, she gasped, tears streaming down her face. Pure determination enabled her to grip the knife as it slid out of her pocket. Pressing the automatic button, she gasped again as she heard the opening click. Working carefully so as not to drop the knife, she began to sever the rope. She must finish before Phil lit the fuse and came running back to carry her off to Canada or join her in certain death. She worked as quickly as possible and just managed to cut through one of the strands of rope when she heard footsteps from deeper in the mine.

"I don't think you've been a good girl," said a voice from the darkness.

The flashlight beam appeared and spotlighted her just as she severed the final strand and freed her hands. "What do you suppose we should do about that?"

Phil slowly raised the SureFire beam and the pistol until both were aimed directly into Cynthia's face.

She closed her eyes and prayed.

CHAPTER TWENTY-FIVE

"THEY MUST HAVE GONE into the mine. Why else would the Jeep be hidden here? I need to go after them. No telling what he might do to her. You stay here with the horses."

"The horses will be fine without us. You're not going in there alone. There's a flashlight in my saddle bag and first aid equipment if needed."

Rather than arguing, Ron nodded. His lack of preparation for a mountain rescue reminded him again of the gap between them. He didn't stand a chance of mounting a rescue without Penny's help. He wouldn't have even been able to find the mine without her. Accepting the flashlight she pulled out of her pack, he climbed over the rocks scattered in front of the dark opening in the hillside and entered the mine.

They moved cautiously over the scattered rubble of fallen timbers and dumps of waste rock material. The site obviously qualified for the newly announced Superfund program as a hazardous locale. Evidence of drilling and blasting remained in the form of detritus dispersed over the floor, making each step an exercise in vigilance. He realized they had no way of knowing how far ahead Phil might be. Even the kicking of a stone could alert him of a pursuit, putting Cynthia in even greater danger. Not finding them would leave him free to plant the dynamite and dirty bomb, elevating the danger level not just for them, but for all of Yellowstone Park should the scheme of the terrorists succeed. The chance of a blast setting off the super-volcano seemed scant, but the addition of a nuclear explosion raised the bar to a new level. A small nuclear explosion would contaminate the area for years.

Penny grabbed his arm and steadied the flashlight beam, focusing it on a pile of loose rock. "Blood," she whispered.

The red droplets would have been missed without her keen eyesight but having them called to his attention provided even greater incentive to push on into the darkness without regard for his own safety. His worry for his cousin would have been enough to move him to action. Add to that the concern for hundreds of tourists, and the land he had come to treasure. Compound those emotions with the overwhelming love he felt for the girl at his side, rapidly becoming more important to him than life itself. Failure could not be an option.

In a way the entire scenario presented a culmination of all the horrible experiences he faced in life. If he had not been pulled from the graduation line at the Academy, he would not have joined the Certain Sounds. If he had not joined the Certain Sounds, he would never have visited Elk Lodge, Montana. If he had never visited Elk Lodge, Montana, he would never have met Penny Whitman. If the quartet had not disbanded, he would never have returned to Elk Lodge. If he hadn't returned to Elk Lodge, he would never have uncovered the plot by the May 19th terrorists. If he didn't stop the plot—.

As they carefully rounded a curve in the tunnel, Penny grabbed the electric torch from his hand and quickly shut it off. Another light illuminated the scene in front of them. Cynthia hung from one of the ceiling beams by a noose while Phil spotlighted her with his SureFire in one hand and his Glock in the other. A slight noise from Ron caused him to switch both the beam and the revolver in their direction.

Penny darted to the opposite side of the mine from Ron and turned on her flashlight again, aiming it directly at Phil's eyes.

"You might as well give up, Adams. You can shoot at the light, but you'll never take both of us. Besides, you're nowhere near the caldera. It's more than three miles before you even get to the edge of the park. Another dynamite blast down here will do nothing to Reagan's campaign. You've lost."

Phil shot twice in the direction of the new flashlight, and it blinked off.

"Penny," gasped Ron. "Are you alright?"

This time the bullet ricocheted off the wall of the cave behind Ron as Phil shot wildly into the darkness at the sound of his voice. Then the flashlight beam bounced off the floor of the mine as he turned and ran toward the dynamite he had planted.

"Go after him," shouted Penny. "He hasn't lit the dynamite yet unless it's a very long fuse. He'd be running the other way if that were the case. I'll get Cynthia."

Penny rushed to where Cynthia hung, and swiftly cut the noose with her own knife. Handing the flashlight to Ron, the girls began the slow trek up to the mouth of the mine in the dark, feeling their way over the rocks and timbers. They traveled only a few hundred feet before an explosion rocked the entire mountainside.

CHAPTER TWENTY-SIX

PENNY WRAPPED HER ARMS around Cynthia to protect her from falling debris as well as to comfort her in the face of their shared worry for Ron. They heard no more gunshots, but knew Ron followed close behind Phil in his attempt to prevent the bombing. She had no way of knowing how much of the ancient mine would collapse from the explosion, so she urged the younger girl to as much speed as possible in the darkness. A determination to bring her friend to safety took precedence over fear for the man she finally realized she loved. The fact that her heart continued to battle with her brain for dominion in that regard required continual enlistment of reinforcements in the frustration of what to do about that love.

The disparity of their family heritage would not please her father. He didn't want her dating young men from the other tribal backgrounds, so what would he say about a white man?

The geographical distance between Montana and Washington, D.C., seemed insurmountable. She felt as if they came from completely different countries.

Their diverging life goals failed to coincide. His great desire to return to the FBI Academy clashed sharply with her pursuit of election as Governor of Montana.

The contrast of religious backgrounds. She was a first-generation Christian, while his family had been part of the church for generations.

The contrast of cultural traditions. The list went on and on.

As they stumbled over the wooden cribbing and shaft decking left behind by Fairweather and his partners, those reinforcement troops preventing the admission of her love faded away into the background. None of those differences mattered. Her heart proclaimed a love which her brain could not dispute. A man who would rush into danger to protect family had a heritage not at all unlike hers. He may have been raised in Washington, but his dedication to the preservation of the West shone like a sunrise over snow-capped mountain peaks. His goal to defend his country mirrored her vision for her state like the reflection of Aspens on a quiet lake. Religious background had brought them both to the foot of the cross. The search for Cynthia required input from both of their cultural traditions.

She loved him. And now he was gone.

The bright sunlight at the opening of the mine's headframe pulled them out into the meadow where the horses waited. Cynthia collapsed onto the grass, tears welling out of her eyes.

"He's gone, isn't he." It was a statement, not a question.

"We'll send someone back to see. Right now, we need to get you to the hospital. According to Ron there's a strong possibility of radiation exposure for both of us."

Penny knew her only option was to keep moving or she would be lying right there next to Cynthia on the grass unable to stir because of despair. They couldn't let Phil do any more damage than he had already managed to accomplish.

"We can call the ranch and your home from the hospital. But we can't risk contaminating anyone else. I'll take the horses. Will you be able to drive the Jeep?"

Cynthia struggled to her feet, wiping away the tears. "Whatever it takes. You're right. We need to go even though what I would like to do is head back into the mine to find Ron. I can drive." Impulsively, she threw her arms around her best friend. "By the way, thanks for coming to get me. I'm not sure how much longer I would have lasted with that rope around my neck."

Penny returned the hug and then grabbed the lead rope from Ron's horse and swung into Geronimo's saddle. "I'll follow you in case you have trouble with the Jeep."

All the way down the mountainside she argued with herself. The importance of getting Cynthia to the hospital weighed heavily on her conscience, but she felt guilty for not going back into the mine after Ron. The chance of him escaping the collapse was slim. That truth had to be accepted. Convincing her heart to accept the fact that he was gone forever would take far more time. Whoever said that time healed all wounds must never have known what it meant to recognize love and lose love in a single hour.

When they reached the ranch road, she waved Cynthia down. "Let's take the horses back to the corral and ride into town together. Maybe Dad and your father have returned."

Cynthia simply nodded agreement, further assuring Penny of the wisdom of her decision. She feared the young girl might be going into shock. It wouldn't do to have her driving the Jeep any longer than necessary.

Back at the ranch the two of them turned over the horses to Wicasa, Alicia's husband and Lee's right-hand man. Penny offered a brief explanation which he accepted without question, promising to give word to James and Lee as soon as they returned. Penny knew Wicasa would brush the horses down, bring them fresh hay, wipe the saddles with saddle soap, and rinse off the pads. Normally she would never have turned that task over to anyone else, but the trip to the hospital demanded precedence over every other task.

During the trip into town, silence prevailed. Cynthia curled up in the passenger seat, occasionally wiping the tears from her eyes. An encyclopedia of words and phrases raced through Penny's mind, none of them adequate or appropriate for the occasion. The healing balm of a solitary ride down the winding trails of their own personal grief brought comfort no words could express.

The hush ended as soon as they walked into the Emergency Room. At the mention of possible contamination, a nurse directed them to the showers. Clothes were removed from head to toe with all personal items placed into a property bag. The nurse labeled the bags with their names, date and time of the collection, the hospital address, and a radiation warning label. All the time she carried on an itemized narrative of the process to be followed.

"Removing clothes and shoes reduces contamination by up to ninety percent," the nurse informed them. "Your belongings will be stored in a secure location, but I must inform you that it may be necessary to dispose of them. Don't use hot water, keep it lukewarm. The soap is mild, but you will need to use it everywhere, including in your hair. Protocols call for two complete soapings and rinsings. Even so, radioactivity trapped in the outer layer of your skin may remain up to two weeks until sloughing occurs."

Nearly an hour passed before they were finally admitted to a room, dressed in uncomfortable waterproof gowns which the nurse told them "were necessary to limit the spread of contamination to their immediate environment as well as to other people." Another radiation warning label had been placed on the door, with access permitted only to authorized personnel. That did not include Elizabeth and Will, who had raced to the hospital in response to a call from the admissions desk. Penny could clearly hear Cynthia's mother through the closed door.

"I know what you are saying. But that's my daughter in there. I understand your rules. But can't you at least open the door and let me see her?"

The negative response of the nurse was offered in a muted voice. The door remained shut.

Elizabeth collapsed into a chair in the hallway, with Will providing her only comfort by means of a hand on her shoulder. He had no idea how to deal with a mother's tears.

Before the nurse could re-enter the girl's room in her hazmat suit, a stentorian, alto voice spoke authoritatively as a woman strode down the hall flashing a badge.

"Ethel Planck, FBI. You might as well let them in. There's no danger of radiation. The reports of a dirty bomb were a hoax. I'll take the responsibility with your supervisor."

The response from the nurse faded into the background as Elizabeth rushed into the hospital room followed by Will. Through the open door, Penny could hear the instructions given to the nurse by the librarian with the FBI badge.

"Find a doctor to care for their real injuries. I understand your protocols and am thankful you have followed them. But I assure you, there is no radiation involved. It is safe to treat them just like any other patient."

As Ethel followed Elizabeth and Will into the room, she approached the two beds with a smile. "We've been in touch with your father, Penny. Lee and Rev. Freeborn are on their way to the mine even now."

Penny fought back tears. "If we had only known there was no radiation, we would never have left Ron," she cried. "There was an explosion. I didn't know if the entire mine would collapse. Ron told me about the bomb, but we would have gone back to try to rescue him. We should have gone back."

Ethel shook her head slowly, laying a hand gently on Penny's arm. "You did what was right for Cynthia, Penny. You're not the only one convinced Phil had a dirty bomb. He thought so himself. Those who sent it to him were just as deceived as everyone else. Scientists came up with the hoax in order to convince Moscow they were making great discoveries and needed more funding. From the beginning the story took on a life of its own. Phil's contacts back east swallowed the myth and purchased a worthless pile of junk, thinking they possessed nuclear material. The great Russian disinformation apparatus strikes again."

CHAPTER TWENTY-SEVEN

PRESS RELEASE

EXPLOSION IN YELLOWSTONE NATIONAL PARK.

THE FAILED ENVIRONMENTAL POLICIES OF PRESIDENT RONALD REAGAN AND SECRETARY OF THE INTERIOR JAMES WATT HAVE SUCCEEDED IN DESTROYING A NATIONAL TREASURE. EARLY THIS MORNING AN EXPLOSION ROCKED THE PARK AT THE SOUTHWESTERN EDGE OF THE CALDERA. ILLEGAL EXPLORATION OF OIL, GAS AND MINERAL RESERVES IN THE AREA HAVE BEEN ALLOWED BY THIS ADMINISTRATION IN SPITE OF THE DANGER OF DESTROYING LOWER GEYSER BASIN, BLACK SAND BASIN, AND OLD FAITHFUL. A POTENTIAL NUCLEAR EXPLOSION THREATENED TO SET OFF THE LONG-FEARED SUPER-VOLCANO. NUMEROUS ENVIRONMENTAL AGENCIES ARE CALLING FOR THE IMMEDIATE RESIGNATION OF THE PRESIDENT.

LENARD FERGUSON, A SUMMER intern for the *New York Times*, opened the hand-delivered press release and immediately brought it to the attention of one of the editors. Recognizing the importance of the story, and under pressure to publish a possible scoop before the competition, Dan Bledsoe considered briefly the possibility of simply printing the release as an exclusive. Instead, he followed journalistic procedure and began his search for independent confirmation. Within minutes a telephone call had been placed to one of his contacts at ATF in Washington, Greg Levenson.

"Alcohol, Tobacco and Firearms. This is Levenson speaking."

"Greg. Dan Bledsoe from the New York Times. What can you tell me about an explosion in Yellowstone Park?"

Judson Freeborn heard only one side of the conversation, but what he heard sent him to another line for a long-distance call to Ethel Planck in Montana. Others in the ATF office tried to piece together the facts from what they overheard from the two men on their phones.

Greg started taking notes as he communicated with Editor Bledsoe. "Yellowstone Park? Where did you receive such a report?"

Judson heard someone answer at the first ring. "Ethel? Freeborn here from the D.C. office. What do you know about an explosion in Yellowstone Park?"

"Press release from the Armed Resistance Unit?" said Greg.

Judson laid one hand over the receiver and called across the room to his assistant, "Listen to this Greg. My niece and a friend just reported into the hospital in Elk Lodge with a story about a mine explosion not even an hour ago. How did the New York Times pick up on it?"

Greg acknowledged the question and relayed it to his contact. "You heard about it this morning, Dan? Through a hand-delivered press release? Someone must have known about it in advance."

Judson listened intently and then called again to Greg. "Tell the paper there's no report of any damage outside the mine. No damage to Yellowstone Park at all."

Greg nodded and resumed his conversation. "Dan, we are in contact with the FBI in Montana. No damage to the park, I repeat, no damage to the park. Seems hokey to me for you to get a press release if the explosion just happened. Tell you what, Dan, give us a couple minutes and I promise to get right back to you. You'll have the exclusive as soon as we know the truth."

Greg hung up the phone and then watched as a kaleidoscope of emotions flashed across his partner's face, still listening on the other line.

"They left without Ron?" Judson asked.

After that question, he sat silent as the voice on the other end of the line detailed the events of the day. Once the conversation had come to an end, he tried to share the account with Greg calmly, wanting nothing more than to climb on a plane and head out to Montana to check on his son.

"This Adams guy Ron told us about kidnapped my niece, Cynthia. She's safe. In the hospital though. He made her guide him to an old, abandoned gold mine. Had a crate with some dynamite and what he thought was a dirty bomb, nuclear material. It's what ARU bought from the Barnadsky Institute, just like we thought. The same crate our men saw loaded into that van in New York ended up in Montana. Ron and this girl named Penny rescued Cynthia. Penny took her to the hospital. But they left Ron behind. Ethel says he ran further into the mine to try to stop the perpetrator. My brother James and Penny's father headed back to the mine. The girls rushed to the hospital because of radiation contamination, but they left without Ron. They left Ron behind."

Greg sighed. "They heard an explosion, Judson. Dynamite. You know they had to get out. The girls thought it was a nuclear bomb. I'm sorry."

"Ethel said she would keep us informed. An explosion in an old abandoned mine. No damage to Yellowstone Park. That's good news. We need to stay on top of this, Greg. Dig up that information we discovered about the Varsukov deception and share it with the Times." Judson rested his elbows on the desk and buried his head in his hands. "I need to call Marilyn. How am I ever going to tell Marilyn? They left Ron behind."

An hour later editor Dan Bledsoe received another exclusive press release, this time via email from Washington.

PRESS RELEASE

ALCOHOL, TOBACCO AND FIREARMS, WASHINGTON, D.C.

A MEMBER OF THE MAY 19TH TERROR ORGANIZATION PERISHED TODAY IN A SUICIDE BOMBING INTENDED TO DAMAGE YELLOWSTONE NATIONAL PARK. PHIL ADAMS SET OFF AN UNDERGROUND EXPLOSION NEAR THE SOUTHWESTERN EDGE OF THE CALDERA. REPORTS OF ACTIVITY BY OIL, GAS, AND MINERAL EXPLORATION HAVE BEEN PROVEN FALSE. A SIMILAR REPORT OF A NUCLEAR DIRTY BOMB IS ALSO UNTRUE. THE BOMB IN QUESTION CAME FROM THE BARNADSKY INSTITUTE OF GEOCHEMISTRY, THE SAME INSTITUTION WHICH PROVIDED THE BOGUS CLAIMS GORBACHEV USED TO CONVINCE THE WORLD TO SIGN THE START TREATY. DISCREDITED AND DEPOSED SCIENTIST ZALERY VARSUKOV INVENTED WHAT HE CLAIMED WAS A PINT-SIZED NUCLEAR DEVICE IN ORDER TO CONVINCE THE SOVIET LEADERS THEY WERE MAKING BRILLIANT ACHIEVEMENTS. THE CLAIM WAS FALSE. ONCE AGAIN, A POTENTIAL ATTACK ON OUR AMERICAN WAY OF LIFE BY DOMESTIC TERRORISTS HAS BEEN THWARTED BY THE QUICK ACTION OF A TRUE AMERICAN HERO, RON FREEBORN.

Bledsoe's caution at the *Times* paid off. A front-page exclusive took shape as he typed. Independent confirmation had been received, and he gladly gave credit to ATF agent Greg Levenson as he wrote the article, including within it the information from the Washington office.

The article did not mention the fact that Ron was still missing.

CHAPTER TWENTY-EIGHT

RON AWOKE TO A pain in his legs, something he experienced with mixed emotions. Pain meant he was still alive. It also meant he lay trapped by falling rock. The flashlight still shone but lay just out of reach. Dust and debris filled the air, making everything appear as if in a fog. Testing the extent of his injuries, he sat up slowly, exploring the condition of his lower body with his hands.

Had the girls made it out alive? What had happened to Phil? Did the explosion cut off any possible exit for him? Was it possible the geyser basin had been tapped? He couldn't feel any moisture, but that could change quickly if two-hundred-degree superheated water began seeping into the shaft. Piece by piece he started shoving away the rocks he could reach. Even with the pressure relieved, the pain alerted him to what felt like permanent damage. Definitely a broken leg.

It took nearly an hour of painful stretching and lifting to remove all the rock. Finally recovering the flashlight, he shone it deeper into the mine. The collapsed cribbing which once supported the roof clearly answered his question concerning Phil. The explosion designed to affect world events had claimed at least one victim.

Crawling through the rubble on the floor of the mine, dragging a broken leg behind him, and holding the flashlight in his teeth, Ron managed over the next hour to get back to the place where he had left the girls. Relief that they were gone mingled with a realization that they must have thought he was dead. They wouldn't have left him. Unless they were hurt as well and needed medical attention.

Using the supplies from Penny's saddle bag, he wrapped a broken piece of wood next to his leg as a temporary splint. Another board served as a crutch. Fighting off nausea induced by the pain, he forced himself onto his good leg and began the long trek toward the mouth of the mine. Every step required him to shine the flashlight onto the floor to discover a safe place to step. Then, swinging the crutch forward into that spot and carefully moving his good leg to a level spot while leaning on the crutch, he slid the broken one closer. Small pebbles fashioned themselves into potential disasters in the making. Every time the board slipped on a loose rock or his good leg twisted as gravel shifted, his progress halted.

"At this rate I'll never get back for my own funeral," his voice resonated off the walls of the mine. "I won't be able to pull off a Tom Sawyer appearance. And I'm talking to myself. That's supposed to prove I'm crazy. But it sure feels good to hear my own voice."

He knew no one could hear him but talking helped him to feel more alive. Phil managed to set off the dynamite, but the caldera hadn't erupted in a super-volcano, of that he was certain. Water wasn't flooding the mine from the geysers in the park. Penny and Cynthia had escaped. Unharmed, he hoped.

He gritted his teeth, leaned on the improvised crutch, pulled his broken leg behind him, and determined to escape as well, even if it took the rest of the week.

Rev. Freeborn and Lee Whitman had traveled all the way to the top of the Continental Divide overlooking the drainage down into Idaho before deciding no sign of any other vehicle going that way in the recent past could be discovered. The logging trail showed no evidence of disturbance. They stopped briefly at the ranch, heard the account of the girl's visit from Wicasa, and stopped to check the answering machine. The message from Ethel came through. As much as they wanted to head into town to see that the girls were all right, they instead took the turn onto the logging road leading to the mine.

"Doesn't sound good for Ron and Phil." Lee maneuvered his 4x4 around the boulders on the abandoned track. "Adams sure had me buffaloed."

"We all liked him," James agreed. "Cynthia especially. She's not often wrong when it comes to character. Just goes to show the extent to which someone will go for political gain."

"Evil. Pure evil. Guess that's what you've been talking about all these years on our hunting trips."

James nodded. "The heart is deceitful above all things and desperately wicked."

"My people call him the Trickster, always stretching the rules until he gets into more trouble than he can handle. Like the story of the man who could take out his eyes and place them on the limb of a tree to gain an advantage over his enemies. He had been warned not to do it more than four times a day, but he chose to ignore that warning. When his eyes wouldn't come back to him, he complained to the buffalo, who gave him an eye. But the eye of the buffalo wouldn't fit into his socket."

"I love your stories of the Trickster, Lee. Breaking the boundaries of human behavior always brings consequences. And our attempts to solve those problems ourselves always make the situation worse. What your Trickster needed was someone who could give him back his eyesight."

"Like healing the blind man?"

"You have been listening."

"Hard not to when you and Penny keep after me. I'm not ready to accept what you say you believe about the man Jesus. It is so hard to believe that God became a man. Why would God want to experience hunger, pain, sorrow, and death? What is there about humanity which would attract him to become human?"

"Perhaps the need for a guide who knows the only trail which leads back to God?"

Lee sat quietly for a time before answering. "I am more and more convinced that the one we call Wakan and the one you call God are one and the same. The Arapaho doesn't dwell much on life after death, we concern ourselves with the importance of how we die. Death becomes a triumph to the warrior."

James almost whispered his response. "Greater love has no man than this, to lay down his life for his friend."

"Jesus the warrior," said Lee. "I will need to think about that."

Just then Lee spotted the mouth of the Fairweather and pulled to a stop at the bottom of the field of rubble. The two men turned on their flashlights and had started into the mine when they glimpsed another light shining out of the darkness. Around a bend in the tunnel struggled Ron, covered with dust, leaning on his improvised crutch, and grimacing in pain, but very much alive.

"Mr. Whitman," he said. "I've been wanting to talk to you. I want to marry your daughter."

CHAPTER TWENTY-NINE

DESPITE HIS DECLARATION OF intent to marry Lee Whitman's daughter, Ron had not been alone with Penny since racing down the mine tunnel in a futile attempt to prevent Phil from setting off an explosion. His uncle and Penny's father took him directly to the hospital where doctors x-rayed the leg, manipulated the pieces back into their proper positions, and encased his entire lower limb in a cast.

Penny, Cynthia, and almost every other person in town he had ever met, crowded into the waiting room where the nurse who previously tried unsuccessfully to keep people out of the girls' room exerted her authority.

"Two visitors at a time and no more than five minutes," she mandated.

To Ron's frustration, Penny's five minutes always included another visitor, making any follow-up to his previous declaration impossible.

Adjusting to and practicing with the crutches consumed most of the next morning before his release. Back at the Freeborn's, another parade of well-wishers prevented any one-on-one time with the person he most wanted to see. She sat beside him on the couch, touched his hand often to assure herself he really had escaped alive, but they never managed a private conversation.

The word of Ron's survival passed through the streets of Elk Lodge so quickly that a celebration dinner the next evening needed to be moved from the Freeborn residence to the basement of the library to accommodate those who wanted to attend. The Steamroller arranged for the meal to be catered by the Elkhorn Café, compliments of City Hall. Ethel volunteered the space at the library, and Will Freeborn and Ernie Edwards set up the tables and chairs, along with some of the other fellows from Boy's Brigade. Lee Whitman, Alicia, and Wicasa Walks-Softly came from Ab-Sa-Ro-Ka Ranch. Church members passed the word by means of the prayer chain and drove in from miles around. Reporters from the *Outlook* and KELK radio prepared stories they knew would be shared far outside the local area. The attempted bombing of Yellowstone Park made the front page of every paper in Montana and many others across the country.

As usual, the Steamroller promoted himself to the position of emcee. After asking Rev. Freeborn to say grace and thanking the Elkhorn Café and all the workers for their part in preparing for the celebration, he allowed the servers time to deliver the plates of smoked venison, steamed carrots, mashed potatoes, and stuffing. When most of the crowd had finished eating, he began introducing what he called the "major players in our hometown drama."

"Through no fault of our own excellent town council, Elk Lodge became the epi-center of a world-wide plot to set off the long-feared Yellowstone Park Super-volcano," he began. "We are privileged to have access to the latest and most dependable sources of news concerning this amazing phenomenon. Let me introduce to you the chief agent for the Montana branch of the Federal Bureau of Investigation, and our undercover substitute librarian, Ethel Planck. Ethel, show us your badge."

Ethel shook her head in disapproval and sighed loudly at the overly dramatic introduction but walked to the front of the room and turned to face the crowd. She already knew better than to ignore the Steamroller.

"It all began with the negotiations between Russia and the United States concerning the SLCM or Sea Launched Cruise Missiles. Gorbachev had a desire to convince the rest of the world that the START treaty could be enforced without on-site inspections. Any nuclear weapon emits radiation, and one of the Russian scientists came up with a method of detection from a distance previously thought impossible. Gorbachev lauded the discovery and pushed through the START treaty on the basis of this method of safe arms inspections. However, the discovery proved to be a hoax. Under pressure to convince the Soviet leaders that their scientists accomplished brilliant achievements, the claim that gamma rays could be sensed from more than ten kilometers proved false. Not only was the theory disputed, but scientists also conducted independent experiments conclusively proving the claim invalid."

The FBI agent stopped for a quick drink of water and then continued.

"The same hoaxers in the meantime announced another great discovery. They said they came up with a dirty bomb which could be easily transported and ignited with an explosion of dynamite. Tests quickly proved otherwise, but at that point latent Russian capitalism raised its ugly head. Socialists love to denigrate capitalism unless they become the beneficiaries of a free economy. Someone high up in the Soviet leadership realized that marketing dirty bombs to terrorists could result in a substantial financial windfall. After all, if they had to be ignited with dynamite, the chance of evidence surviving remained slim. An explosion would take place, and who was to say whether or not nuclear material had been involved. We have traced the journey of such a supposed dirty bomb from eastern Europe, through New York City, and on to Elk Lodge, Montana. From here it traveled to the abandoned Fairweather Mine and was exploded by Phil Adams. He has been identified as a member of the same terrorist group which bombed the United States Capitol back in 1983. We also suspect Adams as the perpetrator of the accident which led to the death of our beloved librarian, Francis Fenton."

The Steamroller stood and raised the entire crowd to their feet as if they were puppets on a string and he was pulling the ropes. "Let us join in a moment of silent prayer for our beloved colleague Miss Fenton," he intoned. "Pastor Freeborn will be holding her funeral service here in the basement of the library which she loved so well. I know that you will all be welcome to attend."

The announcement of the librarian's death brought tears to the eyes of many in the crowd, and sniffles and blowing of noses marked the entirety of the called-for silence. Miss Fenton had guided almost every person in town through the trails of discovery most advantageous to them in the jungle undergrowth of available literary resources. Her reading lists, particularly appropriate to age groups, formed the basis for summer entertainment, right alongside Bible camp, family vacations, and sleeping out under the stars.

"And now," the Steamroller returned everyone to their seats with the downward sweep of his arms. "Let us hear from the hero of Gallatin County, the rescuer of fair maidens, the protector of our great national park, the most amazing pianist in all the world, our own Ron Freeborn."

The mayor led the applause as Ron reluctantly rose to his feet, balancing on his crutches. When it didn't look at if he would move from where he stood, the Steamroller walked over to him and helped him turn to face the room.

"I couldn't have done it alone." He leaned one crutch against the back of a chair and tugged on Penny's sleeve to make her stand. "Penny's tracking skills led us to the mine. Her quick thinking when shots were fired saved my life. She's the one who rescued Cynthia and led her to safety when they thought there was a danger of radiation. I want all of you to know that Penny Whitman is the most amazing woman I have ever met. And she will make a phenomenal governor of the great state of Montana."

The raucous response which greeted his announcement rivaled the enthusiasm of the convention crowd in Billings. Alicia Walks-Softly and her husband handed "In for a Penny" campaign posters to those who stood near them, and an impromptu parade circled the edges of the room. Even the

Steamroller failed to provide crowd control for nearly ten minutes, instead joining in the shouting and cheering which rolled through the library basement like a flash flood on the Red River. When he could be heard once again, he pulled a folded sheet of paper from his breast pocket and waved it around like a banner.

"Listen to this," he shouted. "Ethel just today received a message from her boss, FBI Director William Webster. An email message from Washington, D.C., sent right here to our own Elk Lodge Library Computer. Ladies and Gentlemen, we have entered the age of the Internet."

As soon as the noise in the room subsided to what he felt to be an acceptable level, the mayor started to read.

> WILLIAM WEBSTER, FEDERAL BUREAU OF INVESTIGATION. PLEASE INFORM PROSPECTIVE AGENT RON FREEBORN THAT HE HAS BEEN RE-INSTATED TO THE ACADEMY EFFECTIVE IMMEDIATELY. HE MUST REPORT TO QUANTICO ASAP.

The celebration which followed that announcement proved even more raucous than the one for Penny. Not even the best efforts of the Steamroller to restore order prevailed on reporters from CBS and NBC. They grabbed the opportunity in the chaos to corner Ron and Penny, dragging them in front of the cameras, looking for the sound bites which would provide lead-ins for their late evening news programs.

Alicia made certain that Penny talked to every media person in attendance, from CBS right down to the reporter from the *Fallon County Times* in Baker, Montana.

Ron just about convinced himself that Alicia kept Penny busy on purpose, to prevent him from accomplishing what persisted as of greatest importance, following up his conversation with Lee Whitman. At the same time, he reminded himself that Alicia knew nothing of his desire. Another tribulation, he thought, another opportunity to grow in patience. By the time Ethel and the Steamroller finished arranging his flight back to Washington and planning the trip to Bozeman to catch his plane, the Walks-Softlys spirited off Penny, and the opportunity disappeared like the splash of a rainbow trout feeding on caddisflies.

CHAPTER THIRTY

THE NEXT MORNING, RON watched in dismay as the Pennymobile made its way north on Main Street toward West Yellowstone. All he could do was wave, along with hundreds of other well-wishers sending Penny Whitman off on the campaign trail. As he stood on the sidewalk in front of the Red Rock Inn, the bus cruised past slowly, carrying her into a future he could not share. Alicia Walks-Softly and the campaign organizers planned rallies on each of the eight Indian reservations as well as appearances in every one of Montana's fifty-six counties. Even the town of Winnett, in Petroleum County, the least populous in the entire state with less than five hundred people, agreed to prepare a welcome dinner for her. The next two months before the election loomed like a whirlwind, blowing away the calendar pages rapidly with gale-force winds.

"Tough," Ron complained to himself.

"What's tough?" Ron answered himself.

"Life."

"What's life?

"*Life's* a magazine."

"How much does it cost?

"Twenty cents."

"I only have a nickel."

"Tough."

Life wasn't fair. He should have been allowed to graduate from the Academy. He was excited to be re-instated, but now the disappointment of that earlier frustration would take him away from Montana just when he wanted to stay. His excitement over the prospect of Penny's campaign for Governor battled his desire to complete the course he had followed since childhood. She belonged to Montana. He belonged to Washington, D.C. He longed desperately to join her in the Pennymobile. He wanted to lead the cheering in Winnet and Plentywood, Baker and Wibaux. Uncle

James could claim that disappointments become His appointments, like it said on the motto on his desktop, but in reality, disappointments were just that—disappointments.

"She left something for you." Cynthia slipped a small, wrapped package into his hand. "I think you'll like it."

Ron launched one more wave toward the disappearing bus and shoved his way back through the crowd to where they had parked Cynthia's Jeep. Almost afraid of what he would find, he stared at the gift, trying to imagine what she might have left.

"You'll never know until you open it." Cynthia leaned against the side of the Jeep. "It's not the end of the world, you know."

"Hah. If it isn't, you can at least see it from here."

Ripping off the brown paper, he gazed at a clear glass bottle of liquid, tightly capped to prevent it from spilling.

"It's pure Montana crick water," Cynthia grinned. "She knows that if you drink it you will come back."

CHAPTER THIRTY-ONE

THE PENNYMOBILE ROLLED THROUGH the streets of Bozeman to the accompaniment of hundreds of honking horns. People waved rodeo posters featuring Penny on Jupiter accepting the crown as Queen of the Home of Champions Rodeo. Newsboys sold papers on every corner with the one-inch headlines "WHITMAN SAVES YELLOWSTONE" prominently displayed.

For the parade route she saddled up and rode Jupiter at the head of the rodeo team from Montana State University, her alma mater. The mayor presented her with the keys to the city. Native American dancers performed in authentic regalia using pipes, fans, whistles, and rattles, to the accompaniment of drums.

Overhead a Western Airlines 737 left a jet-trail in the sky as it headed toward Salt Lake City for a connecting flight to Washington, D.C.

The editorial page in the Bozeman *Daily Chronicle* endorsed Penny Whitman for Governor along with Ronald Reagan for re-election as President of the United States. Pundits across the country already predicted a landslide in the presidential race. Former Vice President Walter Mondale had easily defeated Senator Gary Hart and activist Jesse Jackson for the Democratic nomination. But the strong economic recovery, the end of the recession, and the Reagan revival of national confidence, overwhelmed Mondale's call for a nuclear freeze and ratification of the Equal Rights Amendment.

One small article on the last page of the paper marked the only indication that Penny's campaign might face any significant hurdles on the way to victory in Helena.

A COUNTERFEIT PENNY?

"The current campaign is not the first time Penny Whitman has sought the office of Governor in the state of Montana. Few will remember the Girl's State campaign of 1979, but those who do remember are asking the same questions today which surfaced on that occasion. Could

Whitman have ties with the Native Resistance Movement? Could she be a shill? A counterfeit penny?"

"The Native Resistance Movement has been active for the past forty years, advocating a separate nation for Native Americans composed of large portions of Idaho, Wyoming, and Montana. Government agents have repeatedly warned of ammunition and firearms stockpiles held in reserve for armed uprising among the followers of NRM."

"No concrete evidence of Penny's association with NRM has ever surfaced. However, the prime organizer of both the Girls' State campaign and the current whirlwind state-wide tour, happen to be the same person, Alicia Walks-Softly. The husband of Whitman's campaign manager once appeared on a list issued by Alcohol, Tobacco and Firearms of possible members of the Absaroka Statehood Initiative, an early arm of the Native Resistance Movement. Wicasa Walks-Softly also works as a wrangler for the Ab-Sa-Ro-Ka Ranch owned by Lee Whitman. That ranch happens to be located at the precise center of the proposed rebellion, at the junction of Montana, Wyoming, and Idaho."

"In light of these connections, we call on Penny Whitman to immediately denounce the Native Resistance Movement and its goal of armed rebellion for the purpose of overthrowing the very government office she seeks to win in order to establish the anti-American country of Wy-ho-tana."

The by-line on the article read Liz Mitchell.

At a rally in Livingston the next day, one of the marchers in the parade carried a sign which read "Native Born." A photographer for the Livingston *Enterprise* managed to capture a picture of Penny with the home-made sign in the background.

Although the rally in Yellowstone County would be held in Billings, the Laurel *Outlook* reprinted the picture from the Livingston paper and identified the man holding the homemade sign as Raven Appearing Elk of rural Joliet.

The campaign event in Billings proved to be the largest yet. It included a parade, a fifty-dollar-a-plate dinner with the candidate, and a televised town meeting sponsored by KURL television. Various individuals who previously submitted written questions received permission to ask them in front of a live audience. After several questions about her rodeo experience and the Republican platform, a young man rose to his feet.

"Miss Whitman. If you are elected governor, will you use that office to further the cause of Native Americans?"

Penny smiled and looked directly into the camera as she had been instructed. The television audience took precedence over eye contact with those in the room, according to Alicia.

"Thank you for asking. I am proud of my heritage. My father, Lee Whitman, belongs to the Northern Arapaho tribe and was raised on the Wind River Reservation in Wyoming. We call ourselves 'Inuna-Ina' which means 'our people.' Our family heritage can be traced back many centuries to the Algonquin people of the Great Lakes Region who were here even before Marquette and Joliet. My mother, Esther O'Connor, belonged to the Clan Conchobhair with roots in Ireland. To her, clan meant 'children of the family.' Her ancestors also settled near the Great Lakes several generations past. So, to answer your question, yes, I will seek as Governor to further the cause of our people. I am proud to be Native American and I am proud to be Irish, but I am most proud to be called a Montanan."

Hardin welcomed the Pennymobile with a wild-game feed and rodeo, insisting that Penny mount up and compete in the barrel race, which she won handily.

All 189 registered voters in Winnett, Petroleum County, pledged their support to the Whitman ticket at a backyard barbecue.

A blustery snowstorm sweeping down from Canada nearly canceled the rally in Wolf Point, Roosevelt County. Tire chains brought the rally bus through the drifts and supporters arrived despite the weather. Alicia blamed the weather for the smaller turnout, ignoring the fact that Wolf Point was the hometown of the current governor, Ted Schwinden. By the time they headed west toward Great Falls, the warm Chinook winds melted away what remained of the sudden squall.

The Great Falls *Tribune* ran a front-page story concerning the threat to Yellowstone Park and Penny's involvement in preventing disaster. The letters to the editor included one from Liz Mitchell who claimed that Raven Appearing Elk, whose picture now appeared with Penny in many newspapers, held membership in the Native Resistance Movement as well as supporting the Whitman ticket. The letter again called on Penny Whitman to denounce the NRM.

Twelve counties remained on the itinerary when the Pennymobile crossed the Continental Divide and headed toward Kalispell. Only the Helena *Independent Record* had endorsed incumbent Ted Schwinden, a fact which Alicia again chose to ignore, suggesting to Penny that fifteen years of Democratic leadership in the state house fouled the atmosphere in the state capital. President Reagan was still on track for a landslide election and would definitely have long coattails in conservative Montana.

Penny made the front page of the *Missoulian* on the morning they rolled into town, but not for the right reason.

WHITMAN SUPPORTS SECESSION

"In spite of repeated attempts to persuade gubernatorial candidate Penny Whitman to denounce the Native Resistance Movement, she has refused to make that important announcement. Instead, her campaign has welcomed the support of those who seek secession from the Union."

"Government agents advise us that they have been watching closely the activities of the so-called Native Resistance Movement for years. The publicly stated goal of the NRM involves encouraging Native Americans to participate in local elections in order to improve the living conditions on the reservations. But that public persona hides the true goal and intent of the Movement. Their ultimate goal includes rebellion and secession. The three-state area including Wyoming, Idaho, and Montana is often referred to in their private correspondence as Wy-ho-tana. The roots of the movement date back to the Absaroka Statehood movement of 1939 led by A. R. Swick-ard of Sheridan, Wyoming. Absaroka is a Crow word meaning 'children of the large-beaked bird.' Various government agencies, including the FBI and Alcohol, Tobacco and Firearms, have discovered caches of rifles and am-munition in hunting campsites throughout the area, thought to be held in reserve for the initiation of their armed rebellion."

"What could be more dangerous than a Governor whose hidden agenda involves the destruction of the very state government to which she aspires? Candidate Whitman openly admits being raised on a ranch which epitomizes the conjunction of Wy-ho-tana. The ranch, owned by her father Lee Whitman, is named Ab-Sa-Ro-Ka. Her campaign manager's spouse has a long history of involvement with the NRM. She has refused to denounce the Movement's past violence and future destructive goals. Montana cannot afford to take that risk."

This time the article had no by-line.

The parade down West Broadway in Missoula included all the hoopla of previous rallies including high school bands, native dancers, and more horses than could be counted. At the corner of North Higgins, however, it came to an abrupt halt. Dozens of picketers blocked the intersection holding large posters featuring a photograph of Penny holding the "Native Born" sign which first appeared in Livingston. Somehow, the face of Raven Appearing Elk had been replaced by the visage of the Republican candidate for Governor.

The next edition of the *Missoulian* endorsed Governor Ted Schwinden for re-election.

With the barnstorming tour yet to be completed, Penny headed off to Oklahoma City for the National Finals Rodeo, leaving Alicia to deal with the fallout.

CHAPTER THIRTY-TWO

OUTWARDLY QUANTICO HAD NOT changed in the four years since Ron's attendance. "Fidelity, Bravery, Integrity" still graced the front entrance. The FBI buildings still comprised only a portion of the Marine Corps Base. The first day still featured a one-mile run which had to be completed in under ten minutes.

Ron was thankful for the hiking and outdoor conditioning which had been part of his time in Montana. He knew the physical fitness class would not have been a problem even in two-hour blocks. The fact that he still walked with crutches made the subject moot. Hikes through the mountains with the Boy's Brigade and trail rides with Penny and Cynthia worked muscles no exercise demands would ever equal, but he couldn't overcome the handicap of a broken leg.

Although the buildings and routine remained unchanged, Ron sensed an entirely different spirit among the recruits. The optimism of President Reagan replaced the malaise of President Carter. The release of the Iran hostages after 444 days in captivity restored hope that America could once again be a key player on the world stage. The disastrous withdrawal from Vietnam, essentially surrendering to the Viet Cong communists, now faded into history.

"It's morning in America," the Republican party proclaimed in a television commercial. "Today more men and women will go to work than ever before in our country's history. With interest rates at about half the record highs of 1980, nearly 2,000 families today will buy new homes, more than at any time in the past four years. This afternoon 6,500 young men and women will be married, and with inflation at less than half of what it was just four years ago, they can look forward with confidence to the future. It's morning again in America, and under the leadership of President Reagan, our country is prouder and stronger and better. Why would we ever want to return to where we were less than four short years ago?"

Prouder. Stronger. Better. Ron saw it in the eyes of his fellow class-mates. He sensed it in their walk and heard it in their voices. Every recruit wanted to hear his story of Yellowstone Park. The entire barracks gathered on the evening of the National Rodeo Finals in Oklahoma City to help him cheer on Penny Whitman to victory in barrel racing.

The classes also changed very little. Many of the same instructors re-mained in place, welcoming him back like a conquering hero. Ethics, be-havioral training, forensic science, writing, and investigative techniques still used the same textbooks. Acing the quizzes and tests came easily. Firearms training followed the same procedures he had taught the Boy's Brigade in Elk Lodge. Safe driving had been honed over thousands of miles on the road with the quartet. Real-life scenarios with paint guns paled in comparison to facing Adams with his Glock in hand.

Classes started at 0730 hours, which meant showers began at 0530 when you shared a bathroom with four others. Breakfast opened at 0600 hours, and you needed to be early to beat the rush. By evening, even the hard mattresses looked inviting. News from the outside world filtered in slowly, with that from inside the Beltline taking precedence. Reports from distant Montana proved non-existent. No one on the east coast cared what happened in fly-over country.

Except Ron.

Because the training consisted of review for Ron, he learned on ar-rival at Quantico that he would graduate in October after just eight weeks of classes.

The ceremony, attended by friends and family, would once again be presided over by FBI Director William Webster. Each graduate would be handed a badge and credentials, with special honors awarded for outstand-ing achievement in academics, firearms, and physical fitness. Since he ac-cepted the option of taking the shorter course, Ron didn't qualify for any awards, but that didn't matter. The badge would be all the honor he desired.

None of his present roommates would be part of this graduation, so Ron walked alone across the parade grounds toward the auditorium. The crowds on the sidewalks effectively hid the two men who approached from the opposite direction until they stood right in front of him. Identical Ray-Bans covered their eyes, and a small lapel pin adorned their suit jackets.

"Ron Freeborn?"

"Yes?"

"Come with us please."

CHAPTER THIRTY-THREE

FOR THE SECOND TIME, a military vehicle waited for him at the entrance to the Marine Base. This time his two escorts joined him, one in the back with him and one in the front with the driver. Orders issued from above provided direction, and the trip progressed in silence. Merging onto Interstate 95 North, the vehicle moved quickly toward the Capitol. I- 95 became I-395 as they crossed into the District of Columbia and over the Potomac River. Taking the exit toward the 12th Street Expressway, they merged onto 12th Street and turned right on Constitution Avenue.

Long lines waited in front of the East Wing of the White House, anticipating official tours. Ron and his escorts stopped instead near the West Wing. The agents ushered him along the West Colonnade and into the Oval Office.

Behind the Resolute Desk, which Ron remembered had been made from the timbers of a British navy ship and presented to President Rutherford B. Hayes in 1880 by Queen Victoria, sat the most powerful man in all the world, President Ronald Reagan. A bright sunbeam design on the room-size rug re-enforced his message of morning in America. *Preaching To the Troops*, a painting by Sanford R. Gifford of Union troops gathering to hear a sermon, hung on one wall. Portraits of George Washington and Andrew Jackson, the first western president, graced other walls. Small tables held sculptures, the *Great Saddles of the West, Ol' Sabertooth*, and the *Buffalo Skull*, a memento of President Theodore Roosevelt. Ron knew that Selwa, the wife of Roosevelt's grandson Archie, served as President Reagan's Chief of Protocol. He wondered what she would think of the protocol of bringing a prospective FBI agent into the Oval Office unannounced.

The President rose to his feet as they entered the room.

"Well, if it isn't the Savior of Yellowstone himself. Welcome."

The sparkle in the president's eyes immediately put Ron at ease.

"Mr. President. What a privilege to see you again. I trust your visit to Montana went well." As he leaned across the desk to accept the offered handshake, his eyes noticed a small sign which read, "It CAN be done."

"The privilege is all mine." The President gestured toward one of the chairs which sat near the desk. "I have a special place in my heart for that part of our great country, and especially the Park. Let me tell you a story." He sat down in his chair and leaned back as if they were enjoying a visit together on the back porch.

"Teddy visited the park in 1903 and wanted to experience the wilderness. He insisted that the Secret Service men, his secretary, and even his physician, remain in Gardiner while he toured the park sites. What really irritated the media types was the fact that he left them behind as well. The reporter from the *New York Morning Tribune* grew so agitated that he wrote an article on April 23."

"President Roosevelt on his trip through Yellowstone Park did not fall into a canyon, was not attacked by a bear, was not showered with hot liquid from a geyser, and was not almost lost in the snow. The President needs a new press agent."

"You wouldn't believe how many times I have envied Teddy's behavior that day," finished the President.

When Ron laughed, the President joined him. Head back, a warm smile filling the room, and eyebrows raised, he demonstrated his enjoyment of not only the story but the opportunity to again play the role of an actor and bring enjoyment to an audience of one.

The Secret Service Ray-bans had disappeared from the room. Ron still couldn't relax, sure that some bodyguard must be nearby. Someone must be watching. Could the guardians of the President of the United States really trust anyone enough to leave him alone with them? The days of Teddy Roosevelt venturing alone into Yellowstone Park no longer existed.

Reagan seemed to know what he was thinking. "They're just behind that door." He pointed toward the wall behind the chair where Ron sat. "They really don't leave me alone often, but at least they are sworn to secrecy, unlike the media. That's why I like that story about Teddy so much."

The President leaned forward, giving his complete attention to his visitor. "I would love to take the time to hear the entire story of how you saved the park, but truth be told I am the least free man in the free world. Instead, I am a slave to the agenda placed here on my desk every morning by some anonymous functionary. You and I are now stealing time from the Sultan of Brunei who waits in the Rose Room to present me with an elephant carved from marble. I would love to tell him to substitute a real elephant like the one given to Dwight Eisenhower by the French territories of west-central

Africa, but Selwa and Nancy would both be upset with me. So let me cut to the chase."

Coming out from behind his desk, the President removed a badge from the pocket of his jacket. Ron jumped to attention as President Reagan pinned it to the front of Ron's suit coat.

"I asked Webster for the privilege of performing this task myself. The ghosts who run my life wouldn't give me the time to travel over to Quantico and participate in the graduation, so I decided to bring you here instead. Thought it only fitting to personally undo the mistake created by my predecessor."

"I don't know what to say, Mr. President. What a great honor," Ron stammered.

"The honor is all mine. In my opinion you have served faithfully without the badge, and I know you will serve just as faithfully with the badge."

Returning to his seat behind the desk, the President grinned as if revealing the greatest secret of all.

"I understand there is some political conflagration happening in the state of Montana. Agent Planck in Helena informed us that a certain young candidate for governor has been accused of supporting the Native Resistance Movement. Therefore, I am assigning you to the protective detail of gubernatorial candidate Penny Whitman. I expect you to undertake your duty as soon as you can make the necessary arrangements. Will that be acceptable to you?"

Ron simply grinned in reply.

CHAPTER THIRTY-FOUR

JUDSON AND ELIZABETH FREEBORN and their invited guest, Helen Forrester, sat through their second FBI Graduation exercise without a clue as to what transpired across town in the White House. This time they had no one to question after the ceremony, no idea who Ron's roommates had been during the abbreviated class schedule. His name appeared on the class roster. Director William Webster offered no explanation when Freeborn was skipped over between Frantz and Gomer.

"At least we know the White House had nothing to do with it this time," Judson mused as they drove back to their house in Georgetown. "But it does seem strange. Lightning never strikes twice in the same place except here in Washington."

Helen heard the piano as soon as she opened the car door.

"It's Bach. *Jesu, Joy of Man's Desiring.* I think everything is going to be all right."

The three of them paused on the porch so as not to disturb the performance.

"It comes from a cantata during the Baroque period, one of several hundred which Bach wrote for every Sunday of the year." Helen's comments, offered *sotto voce*, provided almost a choral accompaniment to the piano. "The format is a chorale prelude. The melody can be heard in the long held notes, while the orchestration undergirds it with the elaborate triplets. The composer wrote that 'the aim and final end of all music should be none other than the glory of God and the refreshment of the soul.' I think Ron's soul has been refreshed."

The contemplative notes issuing from the keyboard proceeded at a slow-moving andante, calming the spirit and offering praise in a majestic and dignified manner. Whatever had happened to Ron to prevent his graduation resulted in praise to the Almighty rather than depression or despair.

"The arranger, Myra Hess, called it her own prayer," whispered Helen as the piece came to an end. "She often played it for concerts at London's National Gallery through the dangerous days of World War II. You can tell that Ron is at peace."

As soon as Ron heard the front door open, he rushed to gather his mother into one arm while at the same time proudly pointing out his badge to his father.

"I'm in, a full-fledged agent of the Federal Bureau of Investigation. They took me to the White House, right into the Oval Office. The President himself pinned it on me."

Judson took his turn providing a huge bear hug while Marilyn and Helen stood by with tears streaming down their faces.

Ron shared the entire story of his visit to the White House and investiture by President Reagan over the meal of parmesan chicken and tortellini topped with fresh basil and parsley, which his mother had prepared in celebration of the day. When he came to the part about his assignment to protect Penny, Judson excused himself from the table. A call to the office of the ATF prompted his secretary to make arrangements for a flight from Washington Dulles to Montana.

"Where do you want to land?" he called to Ron from the front room where the telephone table sat.

"I have no idea," Ron responded. "Penny's campaign has rallies in two counties every day. She could be anywhere. I don't even know who to call. Maybe I should fly into Helena and report to Agent Planck to make it official."

"Make that a one-way trip to Helena," Judson instructed the secretary. Then, after a long pause, they heard him continue. "The red-eye flight tomorrow morning will work just fine. Chicago, Salt Lake City, and Helena. Got it."

"Typical schedule." Ron shrugged when his father came back into the dining room. "There's no direct flight into Montana from anywhere except Salt Lake City." The disappointments which haunted him for years failed to even stir up an ounce of resentment over the delay. The peace of Bach's *Jesu* possessed him entirely. All those stops became simply steps on the way back to Penny.

CHAPTER THIRTY-FIVE

THE RALLY IN BEAVERHEAD County met on the campus of Western Montana College. Since Beaverhead composed the largest land area of all the counties in Montana, an entire day had been allotted to the activities. If people drove that far for a campaign event, Alicia knew they wanted their money's worth. And they did drive. Beaverhead had not voted for a Democratic presidential candidate since 1936 when incumbent Franklin Roosevelt defeated Alf Landon.

"We are definitely regaining the momentum lost during the National Finals." Alicia nodded approval of the bright orange vest fringed with white and decorated with stars and horseshoes that Penny wore as she emerged from her sleeping space at the back of the Pennymobile. "Between the national coverage of your rodeo win and the resumption of our barnstorming tour, the polls show us nearly even with Schwinden. I just wish you could have been here to deal with the fallout from the picture in the Missoulian."

Penny sat down at the table and buttered a piece of toast. "We both know that Liz will pull every trick in the book to see me defeated. She's never forgiven you for that phone call at Girl's State, you know."

Alicia laughed. "I'll never forget her face when she walked into the polling place and learned it was too late to cast her vote. I really think she convinced herself that her one vote would make her Governor, even though you won by a landslide."

"Hopefully she has exhausted her bag of tricks. What's the schedule for today?"

Alicia glanced at her list. "Interview at 8:30 on the Western Montana College radio station. Brunch with the Soroptimists at 9:00. Saddle up at 10:00 for the parade through downtown Dillon, followed by a luncheon with community leaders. The afternoon includes a visit to Bannack, the first territorial capitol of Montana, for a wonderful photo opportunity. I believe we have nine reporters from Montana media outlets joining us for that trip, so be prepared to answer questions. Tonight, a final rally in the campus gymnasium."

"And then back to Elk Lodge for the weekend. What a whirlwind."

"Welcome to politics," laughed Alicia. "Do you really believe it will get any easier once you settle into the Governor's office in Helena? By the way, have you heard anything from Ron Freeborn recently?"

"Not since he called to congratulate me on the win in Oklahoma City. He's pretty busy with his studies at the Academy."

"Well, I've been thinking about that, Penny." Alicia sat down across from her friend at the small table. "I know he likes you a lot, but I can see a possible danger in that relationship. It would be detrimental to your campaign to face a rumor about a long-distance relationship with someone in Washington, D.C. People might think you lacked dedication to the task of serving Montana."

Penny grabbed Alicia's sleeve, forcing her to look directly into her eyes, face to face.

"Alicia, you have been a wonderful, loyal friend for many years," she said. "I truly appreciate all that you have done to raise money, schedule my campaign, bolster my candidacy, and promote my political career. I will never be able to repay your kindness and friendship. But when it comes to my personal life, I draw the line. If I thought for a moment that you would do anything to hinder a relationship between Ron and me, I would fire you so fast you would be convinced that you had somehow started roller skating in a buffalo herd."

Alicia threw up her hands as if surrendering and pasted a weak smile on her face. "I've always wanted to roller skate in a buffalo herd," she replied. "I just wondered how things stood between you and Ron. I guess that answers my question. Let's get you over to the campus radio station."

Ron's flight from Salt Lake City arrived in Helena at 10:30 Mountain time. Uncertain of how to even begin searching for the FBI headquarters in the capital city, it pleased him to see Ethel Planck waiting in baggage claim.

"Congratulations." She greeted him with a firm handshake. "I've been requesting additional personnel here in the office for months. Never thought it would come by way of the Oval Office. I understand your immediate task entails providing security for one of our gubernatorial candidates."

Ron grasped the outstretched hand of the agent and shook it just as strongly. "Reporting for duty, Ma'am. Just want you to know that I didn't take that instruction too seriously. I can't imagine that either one of your gubernatorial candidates faces a dire need for security. I'll be glad to serve in any way you need me to serve. But it is great to be back in Montana."

"And we are glad to have you back. Grab your suitcases and we'll talk about responsibilities on our way back to the office. Have you had lunch?"

Over a quick fast-food meal at McDonalds, Ethel made it clear that she took the President's assignment seriously even if Ron didn't.

"I assume you know exactly where the Pennymobile is located on this barnstorming tour the campaign has been making?"

Ron tried not to let his embarrassment show. "Not really. I've been pretty busy, and it's not been easy keeping in touch with her tour bus constantly on the road. Believe it or not, Montana events seldom make the evening news back east. I haven't talked to Penny since she won the barrel racing title in Oklahoma City."

"Well, then, that needs to be our first item of business. How can you protect her if you don't even know where she is? I believe I have Lee's phone number in my Rolodex."

The telephone at Ab-Sa-Ro-Ka Ranch rang more than a dozen times before Ethel gave up. "Must be out with the cattle or maybe fishing," she said to Ron. "Who else can we try? Your uncle?"

"He might know," said Ron, "but I think there might be someone even better informed."

"The Steamroller," both of them said at the same time.

"Elk Lodge Mayor's office," said a familiar booming voice a minute later. "If you're calling to complain about taxes, we only take those calls on the sixth Thursday of the month. What can I do for you?"

"Get off your mechanical bull, Steamroller. This is the FBI calling."

"Ethel Planck. Bless your pea-picking soul. You got a Butch Cassidy or a Harry Longabaugh cornered up there at the capitol and need some help?"

"Neither. I have Ron Freeborn here in my office and we need to know where to find the Pennymobile."

"You have come to the right place. I have the entire itinerary right here on my desk, if I can just find it. Put the kid on the line while I look."

Ethel handed the phone to Ron with a shake of her head. The Steamroller never changed.

"Hello, sir."

"Ron, my man. How's the training going there in Washington? What are you doing in Montana? You didn't get kicked out of the Academy again, did you? We're sure proud of your little gal. Put our burg on the map twice now. First the prevention of the near fiasco in Yellowstone Park, and then a national rodeo title. And she's about to do it again. My old friend Governor Ted is quaking in his cowboy boots, let me tell you. I know I've got it here somewhere. Alicia made certain I had a copy of the location of every rally in the entire state before they left town. Did you know they're visiting every county in the entire state? The entire state. All fifty-six. Plus the reservations. Should be just about done by my reckoning. What's the matter, Ron? Cat got your tongue? I haven't heard a word from you. Let's see. Here it is. Better let me talk to Ethel again. She'll know better where these counties are located. Good to hear from you Ron. Hope you'll be down to see us soon."

Ron laughed as he returned the receiver to Ethel. The Steamroller never changed.

"Why don't you hire a secretary to make sense of that mess on your desk, old man?" Ethel winked at Ron as she took the phone.

"My chaos is organized chaos, mark my words. A secretary would just throw away something I've been saving for years until the day I need it. Beaverhead County. They're down in Dillon all day. You taking Ron down there? Tell you what. The mayor is a friend of mine. I'll give him a call and a heads-up. In fact, I'll do one better than that. I'll make arrangements for Ron to open the rally tonight with a concert. Wouldn't that be a hoot to see little Penny walk into the auditorium to the accompaniment of *I've Been Everywhere?* What I wouldn't give to see the expression on her face. In fact, I will do just that. Wouldn't miss it for the world. I'll see you in Dillon tonight."

Before Ethel could respond, he slammed down his receiver. Her attempts to call him back resulted in a busy signal. He was already on the phone with the mayor of Dillon.

"I hope you brought some music along, Ron. You're going to be playing a concert at the Penny Whitman for Governor rally in Dillon tonight."

CHAPTER THIRTY-SIX

THE PHOTO OP TOUR to Bannack proved to be a rousing success. As Penny stood in front of one of the restored buildings in the ghost town, their guide recounted the story of how an attempt had been made to preserve the first hotel in the territory called the Goodrich House. Light bulbs flashed as each of the reporters took turns with their cameras.

"Mr. and Mrs. Bovey did their best to restore the Goodrich, but deterioration had set in, to the point where very little could be saved. So, instead they moved seven of the porch posts and some of the balcony spindles to Virginia City and re-created the hotel there. The rest of the logs were torn down and used by a local resident to build a chicken coop. Instead of calling their hotel the Goodrich House, the Boveys named it after the discoverer of gold in the Virginia City area, Bill Fairweather."

The reporter from the Bozeman *Daily Chronicle*, who had taken Montana history in high school, immediately recognized that name. "The same Fairweather who dug the mine outside of Elk Lodge?"

"One and the same," said the guide. "He was traveling back here to Bannack from a visit to that mine when he came across the evidence of gold in Alder Gulch, sparking the Virginia City gold rush and the richest gold placer deposits ever discovered. Thirty million dollars in gold eventually came from that fourteen-mile stretch of real estate.""I know you have all heard the story of how Penny saved Yellowstone Park from destruction at the Fairweather Mine," called out Alicia Walks-Softly, quick to take advantage of any positive vibes she could arouse for the campaign. "Penny will be glad to share any details you might have missed."

Cameras flashed and Norelco video handhelds whirred as Penny walked down Main Street of Montana's First Territorial Capitol, once again recounting the events of the unforgettable day which first brought her to national prominence. The background of sixty log, brick, and frame structures, the best-preserved ghost town in Montana, assured Alicia that the news cycle for the next day would prove positive. She almost regretted the necessity of bringing the event to a close when it became time to rush the Pennymobile back to Dillon for the evening rally.

True to his word, the Steamroller made arrangements with the mayor of Dillon to move a grand piano into Main Hall Auditorium on the Western Montana College campus so Ron could provide a prelude to the evening rally. Although the rally had been scheduled for 7:00 p.m., people began arriving over an hour early, afraid seating might be limited.

"No sense letting a good crowd go to waste, Ron," the Steamroller observed. "Give them what you prepared, and I'll start circulating for requests. Did you bring any of those record albums along? People out here love Southern Gospel. The mayor says Penny and her entourage haven't made it back from Bannack yet, but I know you can keep everyone happy until they get here. Just make yourself at home there at the keyboard and let me take care of the rest."

Without waiting for a reply, the Steamroller pushed through the crowd, clearing the way for Ron and Ethel to follow. The noise level in the room would have prevented a reply even if one of them had tried to break into his monologue, so they didn't even make the attempt. Amazingly, as soon as Ron sat down at the piano and struck the first chords of the *Assurance March Around the World,* the noise abated to near silence. Instead of people shoving through the doors and scrambling for seats, they moved quietly into place and sat down to listen. Every gospel song he played elicited enthusiastic applause, and even the Gustav Holst piece inspired appreciation when people started to recognize the sounds of the *Imperial March* from Star Wars.

Between the numbers from Ron's classical training and tour repertoire, the Steamroller placed slips of paper on the music rack with requests from the crowd. Those Ron recognized he added to the concert, and those he didn't know he ignored. Just before 7:00 the latest note read *I've Been Everywhere.* The arrangement he wrote for the Certain Sounds at the National Quartet Convention emerged from the back of his mind and became the song he played as Penny walked onto the platform.

The arrival of the Republican candidate for Governor, accompanied by all the local city and county officials, brought the crowd to its feet. Native American drumbeats resounded from the back of the auditorium. Enthusiastic volunteers clapped in time with the drums. Ron didn't even bother to finish his piece. Closing the piano, he slipped into the nearby seat saved for him by Ethel Planck and joined the rhythmic applause.

Alicia never joined Penny on the platform; her job kept her behind the scenes. When she spotted Ron at the piano, she calculated the angle of approach Penny would make to the dignitary seating area and made an executive decision.

"Wicasa," she whispered, grabbing her husband's sleeve to make sure she had his attention. "Freeborn is here. Take him backstage. I need to talk to him."

With all attention focused on the platform, Wicasa faced no difficulty circling around to where Ron sat, touching him lightly on the arm. Nodding toward the backstage area, he indicated for Ron to follow him. Once there, Alicia directed them both to a storage room just off the auditorium.

"Ron, it's good to see you," she began. "This is a total surprise and I know Penny will want to see you. But I need you to listen and listen closely. We have less than a week before the election. I know you would never do anything to hinder Penny from becoming Governor, but you need to understand that just your being here threatens to do exactly that. She needs to be viewed as totally committed to the state of Montana. If word leaked out that she was dating someone from Washington, D.C., it would be the nail in the coffin that provided the death knell for her candidacy. Do you understand?"

Ron tried to listen calmly. He certainly hadn't returned to Montana to cause problems for her campaign, but what Alicia said didn't really make sense. That is, until you realized that no one knew his side of the story yet.

"But I'm not from Washington, Alicia," he protested. "I've been assigned here to Montana. Just ask Ethel Planck. I have my badge and I'm working out of the FBI office in Helena."

"I don't care where you've been assigned," Alicia practically snarled. "That won't matter to Liz Mitchell. One sight of you alongside Penny will be enough for her to arrive at any conclusion she desires. And her conclusions are never in Penny's favor. I beg of you, Ron. Just five more days. Give us five more days. Come to the celebration in Bozeman the night of the election, and you can have all the access to Penny you ever desired."

As they heard the chair of the Republican party of Beaverhead County introducing Penny as the "next Governor of the great state of Montana," Ron hesitantly nodded agreement.

"Five days," he said. "Just five days."

CHAPTER THIRTY-SEVEN

DESPITE ALICIA'S CALCULATION OF the angles, Penny saw Ron leave the piano and take a seat beside Ethel Planck. Her immediate inclination to jump off the platform into his arms was tempting, but protocol aided her in resisting such action. Instead, she greeted all the guests on the platform during the initial applause and then walked to the podium to recognize the crowd. At that point, the opportunity to glance down at the seats near the piano fit with protocol, but the empty seat next to Ethel puzzled her. Throughout the evening, even while delivering her stump speech, her eyes searched for the one person she most wanted to see. She almost convinced herself that his earlier appearance had been simply a product of what she so much desired, until she ran into the Steamroller while shaking hands after the rally.

"What a night," he practically shouted. "I'm going to instruct the town council to commission a sign to grace the entrance to Elk Lodge. Home of Penny Whitman, youngest Governor of the great State of Montana. Between the National Finals last month and the election next week, you have certainly placed our fair city on the map. And you can thank me for the piano concert. When I heard that Ron returned to Montana to work with Ethel, I just knew we had to get him here for the rally. What a night."

The entire time he expostulated, the Steamroller shook Penny's hand until she began worrying that he would pull her arm right out of its socket. Finally, Alicia tapped hard enough on his wrist to make him release his grip. Before he could begin again, and before Penny could question him about Ron, Alicia turned her in the other direction and introduced her to the chairwoman of the Dillon city council. Next came the state representative from Beaverhead County, then the city librarian, and the Western Montana College chancellor. Before all the introductions ended, the Steamroller disappeared.

They were on their way back to Elk Lodge in the Pennymobile before Penny had a chance to question Alicia. She looked forward to returning home after nearly two months on the road, while at the same time hoping that perhaps Ron would be visiting his uncle in Elk Lodge. Something puzzled her about the way he had disappeared at the beginning of the rally.

"Did you know Ron would be playing a prelude tonight?" she asked Alicia. "Did you know he was back in Montana? Don't you think that would have been something of interest to me?"

"Now, Penny," Alicia shook her head sadly. "You know the Steamroller. I heard about the concert at the same time you did, when I walked into the auditorium, and Ron sat there at the piano. The two mayors took it upon themselves to rearrange the schedule for the evening. I had nothing to do with it."

"But you did have something to do with his disappearance, right?"

The campaign manager closed her eyes and blew several times into her hands as if trying to avoid hyper-ventilating before answering in obvious exasperation. "We have talked about this before. Five days, Penny. The end is in sight. We can't afford any surprises, October or otherwise. Ron agrees with me about this. He's going to stay away until election night."

"So, you and Wicasa?"

Alicia nodded. "We talked to him. He's on his way back to Helena. He'll be working out of the FBI office there under Ethel Planck. He promised to stay away until the celebration in Bozeman the night of the election."

Penny took several deep breaths to calm her spirit, and then stood to her feet and walked toward her room at the back of the bus.

"Five days, Alicia. No matter what happens on election day, in five days you will be without a job. I told you my personal life was off limits. You're fired."

RETURNING TO HELENA WITHOUT talking to Penny loomed large, the hardest mission Ron ever faced.

"I have no idea whether Alicia is right," he told Ethel as she drove back to the capital after the rally. "But she's the expert on Montana politics. I'll just have to wait."

"I'm certain the tension on the campaign trail stands at an all-time high right now," said Ethel. "From what I have observed about Alicia Walks-Softly, she resents any changes to plans she creates. You must admit that she runs a mighty effective campaign on behalf of Penny. On the other hand, I can certainly make arrangements for you to use a department vehicle if you decide to drive down to Elk Lodge tomorrow. The President did say that your first assignment was to protect her, right?"

Ron grinned weakly. "According to Alicia, that means protecting her from me. Thanks for the offer, but no. I made a promise. I need to keep my word."

CHAPTER THIRTY-EIGHT

GREG LEVENSON ANSWERED THE telephone call at the ATF office in Washington the next morning simply because he arrived early, and the secretary didn't.

"Alcohol, Tobacco and Firearms. Levenson speaking."

"Oh, I'm so glad I was able to get ahold of you." The voice on the other end of the line sounded to Greg like a teenage girl running hard and out of breath.

"What can I do for you?"

"I'm not sure. But I just need to tell someone. I saw them just last night, but I don't think they saw me."

"Saw who ma'am? Where were you?"

"Just down the street from where we live. Right here on Wallace Street, just south of the State Capitol. Men. Several of them. I don't know how many. But they had guns. A whole room full of guns. Right here in Helena."

"Helena, Montana? Are you calling from Montana?"

"That's what I said. I didn't know who to call, but I saw that article in the *New York Times* about Yellowstone Park and they mentioned ATF. Is it all right to call you?"

"You've done the right thing, ma'am. Now give me your name and contact information so we can have someone get in touch with you."

A click and buzz on the other end of the line concluded the conversation.

Judson walked in as Greg held the phone out in front of his face, staring at the receiver.

"Phones usually work better if you place them close to your ear," he joked. "It's only in Dick Tracy comics that you can actually look into your phone and see the person who is talking."

"I wish I could have seen her. She wouldn't give me her name, but she sounded scared."

"Scared? About what?"

"Guns. Men with guns. In Helena, Montana. I think we'd better give Ethel Planck a call."

When Ron arrived at the FBI office that morning, Ethel handed him a bulletproof vest and a Smith and Wesson 459.

"Your Dad called," she said. "ATF in Washington received an anonymous call from here in Helena about a cache of weapons over near the Capitol. It may be nothing but someone's hunting collection, but they want us to check it out. Are you ready for your first field assignment?"

"As ready as I'll ever be. Let's go."

Although Wallace Street began near the Capitol, it extended only a few blocks. Armed with nothing more than the information from the anonymous caller, Ethel decided that going from house to house in FBI raid jackets and hats, clearly marked on the front and back, would probably be the quickest way to learn more. They had walked a little more than a block when a young girl approached, almost as if she had been waiting for them.

"Are you from the FBI?" she said.

Ron nearly groaned at the question. They couldn't have been more clearly identified if they had been accompanied by a brass band playing the theme from *Dragnet*. But Ethel smiled and answered for both of them. "That's right. Just following up on a lead we received. Checking on any unusual activity near the Capitol before election day. Do you live near here?"

"Just up the street. I'm the one who called ATF. It's that house over there, the one with the For Sale sign." As quickly as she appeared, the girl ran off, seemingly afraid of retribution for talking with them.

Ethel wrote down the number of the Realtor whose sign had been planted in the front yard. "We'll call and ask for a key," she told Ron. "The house is obviously empty." As they drove back to the office to make the call, Ron decided that people out west must be more inclined to cooperate with law enforcement. He couldn't imagine anything like this happening back Washington, D.C. Casually walking down a sidewalk in Georgetown would be more likely to make them a target for a sniper than an informer.

When the key arrived, Ethel knocked loudly before entering and then led the way into the basement.

"Bolt action, lever action, and a few semi-automatics," said Ron, surveying the small piles of rifles scattered around the basement floor. "No Uzis or machine guns or grenades. Looks more like what you would find in a hunting camp."

Ethel agreed. "I'll have the office send over a cargo van and we'll take them into custody. The only unusual factor is the location. What are they doing in the basement of an empty house?"

The answer to that question came with the arrival of the Sunday edition of the *Helena Independent Record* the next morning. To his amazement, Ron made the front page. Someone had taken a picture just as he placed an armful of rifles from the empty house into the back of the FBI van. The headline read:

FBI CONFISCATES NRM WEAPONS CACHE

"An anonymous tip to the ATF resulted in a major discovery for the FBI on Saturday. A large cache of weapons, believed to belong to the Native Resistance Movement, was confiscated from a safe house just minutes from the State Capitol Building in Helena. The NRM has been a strong supporter of Penny Whitman in her bid for the governorship, leading many to conclude that the purpose of the arsenal could have been an attempt to initiate the movement's goal of an independent Native American nation called Wy-Ho-Tana. Repeated calls for candidate Whitman to repudiate the secessionist aims of the NRM have met with continued resistance."

The article went on in that vein for two full columns, repeating once again the history of the NRM, the location of the Whitman ranch, and the supposed danger a Native American governor would present to the state of Montana.

The by-line gave credit to Liz Mitchell.

Monday editions of the *Missoulian, Billings Gazette,* and *Great Falls Tribune* shared even more details concerning the raid, identifying the man in the picture as none other than the same Ron Freeborn who prevented the destruction of Yellowstone Park.

Numerous attempts by reporters to contact either Penny Whitman, or her campaign manager Alicia Walks-Softly, failed. The FBI office in Helena remained closed over the weekend, preventing further information from that source as well.

Liz Mitchell's timing proved perfect. She had manufactured her own October surprise.

CHAPTER THIRTY-NINE

VOTING BOOTHS IN MONTANA opened at 8:00 a.m. on the morning of November 6, two hours later than on the east coast. By the time of the evening news, pundits already called the election for incumbent President Ronald Reagan.

Ron arrived at the site of the Whitman rally in Bozeman before the doors opened to the Grand Ballroom. The Pennymobile occupied a prominent place in front of the historic Baxter Hotel. Red, white, and blue bunting decorated the entrance. Television sets throughout the lobby displayed views of all the major network news programs. Dan Rather on CBS. Tom Brokaw on NBC. Ted Koppel on ABC.

When staff opened the doors to the ballroom, well-wishers quickly filled the room, joining the television crews and reporters granted early access to set up their equipment. Tables loaded down with doughnuts, bottled water, bowls of mixed nuts, and plates of fresh fruit lined the walls. Volunteers in blue moved through the crowd distributing "In for a Penny" signs, small American flags, "Whitman for Governor" buttons, and plastic cowboy hats with a picture of Penny riding Jupiter on the front. A grand piano sat unopened to one side of the stage, surrounded by a Native American drum circle, warming up for the dance troupes scheduled as part of the entertainment for the evening.

As Ron looked around for a familiar face from Elk Lodge, he spotted the one person he had no desire to see, Alicia Walks-Softly.

"Well, if it isn't Mr. FBI himself," Alicia's eyes sparked and darkened with distaste. "You just can't resist getting your picture in the paper can you. I suppose I should thank you for staying away from Penny for five days, but I wish you had stayed away from Montana entirely. You do realize, I hope, that your little escapade in Helena may cost her the election."

"Hello to you too, Alicia," said Ron. "You do realize, I hope, that the entire story was sucked out of some reporter's thumb. We found no evidence of NRM involvement. In fact, we found nothing at all except a collection of hunting rifles in an empty house."

Alicia laughed bitterly. "The mighty FBI has been snookered. Snookered. Of course you didn't find anything else. You weren't meant to find anything else. It was a set-up, and you fell for it. Pretty boy Ron Freeborn once again proves his status as a hero. Never mind that his heroism came at the price of destroying the future of the person he claims to love. In politics, every election-night party becomes either a gala jubilee or a depressing funeral. Do you really think you'll be welcome here when this one becomes a wake?"

"I'm sure you have used everything in your political portmanteau to prevent that from happening, Alicia. Now that I've kept my promise to stay away for five days, can you tell me how to find Penny?"

"Afraid not," Alicia said over her shoulder as she walked away. "I've been fired."

EVEN BEFORE THE POLLS closed in the President's home state of California, the Reagan's landslide victory became obvious. By late evening all the news anchors agreed that he prevailed in every state of the union except Walter Mondale's home state of Minnesota.

The returns from across Montana came in much slower than the national vote. Even so, it soon became clear that the President's coattails had not been long enough to change the existing political landscape in Big Sky Country. One of the most conservative states in the union retained Democratic leadership while supporting Republican control in Washington. Penny's first appearance in the Grand Ballroom that evening came when she walked down from the suite where she had been waiting to give her concession speech. Even so, she greeted the crowd with a big smile.

CHAPTER FORTY

NERVOUS ANTICIPATION OF THE wake Alicia predicted had descended early on the crowd in the Baxter Hotel. Returns from Missoula County and Yellowstone County, two of the largest population centers, indicated nearly a seventy percent lead for Governor Schwinden. Cascade County with Great Falls, and Lewis and Clark County with Helena, returned even larger margins. The smaller counties didn't have enough population to overcome those numbers from the big cities.

People began drifting away soon after the first returns flashed on the television screens in the ballroom. The Black Hawk Performance Company and the Been Nah Un Den Nah Drum Group, brought in from the Chicago American Indian Museum, managed to create their own excitement and animate the enthusiasm of those who remained. The crowd cheered wildly when the chairman of the Republican Party in Montana introduced Penny. But cheers turned to tears as she stepped in front of the microphone to offer her concession and announce that she had already called the Governor with congratulations on his victory.

With that announcement, the slow departure soon escalated into a flood. Many crowded around the platform to shake Penny's hand one more time, give her a hug, and tell her she could count on them anytime in the future. But no one outside the room witnessed that as the lights on television cameras faded and technicians packed up their equipment. Reporters who saw no need for exit interviews soon disappeared. The room which once reverberated with action, color, and excitement turned gray and gloomy.

Only some of the hotel staff remained when Penny offered her last farewells to supporters and became aware someone was playing softly on the grand piano. Walking slowly toward the sounds coming from the keyboard, she took a seat on the bench beside the performer.

"*O the Deep, Deep Love of Jesus* in the style of J. S. Bach's *Jesu, Joy of Man's Desiring*," she said. "I'm Penny Whitman."

146

"Ron Freeborn," he replied, draping one arm across her shoulder while delivering a kiss four years in the making. "Thanks for the crick water."

A waxing gibbous moon illuminated the highway through the Gallatin Valley as they headed back toward Elk Lodge.